T0157465

INTERDIMENSIONAL TRAVEL FOR DUMMIES

A Novel

JOHN LEE BUNTING

Interdimensional Travel for Dummies
A Novel

iUniverse books may be ordered through booksellers or by contacting:

iUniverse
1663 Liberty Drive
Bloomington, IN 47403
www.iuniverse.com
1-800-Authors (1-800-288-4677)

ISBN: 978-1-4917-6459-6 (sc)
ISBN: 978-1-4917-6461-9 (hc)
ISBN: 978-1-4917-6460-2 (e)

Print information available on the last page.

iUniverse rev. date: 04/13/2015

PROLOGUE

Interestingly enough, the world is exactly as it seems—to the untrained eye, of course. But to those who actually know what is going on, it is much more unpleasant than having salt poured into one's eyes while visiting the optometrist. Of course, if salt is being poured into your eyes, I'd recommend getting another doctor.

Now close your (hopefully salt-free) eyes, and try to imagine a world that is highly similar to yours but where everyone is on fire. It is hot, isn't it? In this world of flames, you, having come from your own dimension, are not in flames. Wish you had brought water? Me too. You are sweating a lot. A quick note: this demonstration doesn't apply to those people of Dimension-1143666 because they are burning already. Are you wondering why? It's a dimension of cooking, and everyone has to start somewhere.

You stand amid the burning embers and tormented skies. People on fire wave gingerly to you as they go about their days, doing things that people on fire tend to do. You think to yourself, *Why didn't I read that* Interdimensional Travel for Dummies *book?* Well, it is too late at this point because fire people don't read; they burn things. Amazingly enough, they haven't come up with burn-proof paper.

Dimension traveling is not for the faint of heart or head. It requires a full understanding of the methods of travel and places that will be visited. Anyone who does not choose carefully could end up in a dimension that has some quirk that would drive him or her insane.

Are you a fan of music? Are you a big fan of music? Could you stand being a fan many times greater than what you are thinking right now? We are talking about enduring a 24/7 music-a-thon with music mixed and mingled together to form mind-numbing, repetitive beats that will never leave your head. If you are already covering your ears after just reading this description of the dimension, then you will not want to visit Dimension-3092123. That is, unless you are covering your ears for another reason and do like music. If that is the case, then you should visit this dimension because you get your own theme music that plays differently depending on which way you move.

I'm sure by now some of you are wondering when I'll talk about other dimensions in detail, maybe discuss their identifiers and what to expect in each one. But in order to do that, I would need a long time and perhaps another book. You know what—that is a good idea for another book.

Seeing as I'm now writing a book regarding the many different dimensions, I've decided to remove all earlier ideas from my head and instead tell the story of a youngish man I met once. Don't be angry! This guy was an idiot, and this book title still holds. Anyway, I learned of his story through watching him from afar. Also, I may have met him a few dozen times and perhaps even gave him advice once or twice.

He came from a dimension of normality—or, in terms of interdimensional travel, a Control Dimension. Many of you who read this will probably be from his dimension, seeing as I asked him to take a few copies back with him to distribute.

CHAPTER 1

With a crash, Jason fell out of his vehicle, having misjudged the first step. He landed hard on the warm road but was quick to gain his footing. Brushing himself off, he pointed his finger accusingly at a young woman who sat still in the passenger seat of the vehicle he had just vacated. She wore conservative clothing and had lovely permed blonde hair.

"What did you do!" Jason shouted.

He took a few steps back, and the young woman's lips quivered as he did so. Drivers honked their horns at Jason as they drove around him.

What was going on? Just a few minutes ago Jason understood everything in his life. Now he felt as if his life had been inverted. He was no longer wearing his usual jeans and T-shirt but rather was dressed in all black. His wrists were now covered with leather bracelets. A chain hung from his back pocket, and he swore he was wearing eyeliner.

"Jason! Please get back in the car!" the young woman pleaded.

Jason recognized the source of the voice to be his younger sister, Cara. She looked so different from the way she normally did that he had hardly registered it was her. Usually, she was wearing a short, skimpy outfit, but now her clothes covered most of her skin. Had she been the cause of all of this?

Jason took a few more steps back, pulling at his shirt as if trying to rip it off. First he realized he didn't have the strength to do this, but then he realized that something else was on his wrist besides the leather bracelet. It was a calculator watch, a particular watch that he recalled obtaining earlier that day.

"How did it get wrapped around my wrist?" Jason whispered to the air. His eyes narrowed as he looked at the little screen on the watch where numbers would appear. There was a number there, but not one he ever recalled entering. *Three*, Jason read in his head. The number decreased to a two and finally to a one.

Jason reached a finger out to touch the calculator pad on the watch, but before he could reach the button, he felt sickness come over him. His stomach wretched, and his body seemed contorted as if it were being shoved into a small box. This discomfort wasn't new to him, because he had felt it only minutes before.

Jason took a knee, holding his gut. He staggered a bit, using a hand to keep from toppling over. After a few seconds, he could once again hear things around him. There was the honking of cars, the yelling of people, and the sound of footsteps landing on pavement. He checked both of his wrists and saw no leather bracelets. He checked his shirt and pants as well, and they were back to normal.

On the ground in front of him lay the same calculator watch that had been on his wrist. Its screen was blank. Jason picked up the watch, looked it over, and placed it in his pocket. He stood up and took a step back.

"Well, that was an interesting trip—"

Jason's voice was cut off as a car hit him. He wasn't struck overly hard, as the driver was being careful due to Jason being in the middle of the road, but the impact was hard enough to knock him off his feet and to the ground. It was hard enough that when he opened his eyes after the hit, he could only see the blurred outline of a woman coming toward him. She looked to be in a skirt with a low-cut shirt. His eyes closed, and in his final moments of consciousness, Jason's mind raced over the events that got him here.

CHAPTER 2

It took quite some time for Jason's eyes to adjust to the sunlight that now filled his bedroom. Had he been asleep that long? Jason yawned and stretched before rolling back on his side and pulling his navy-blue comforter to his chin. This was just another day to him. What was the rush?

As sleep once again began to take over Jason, the door to his bedroom burst open, and a tantrum entered the room in the form of his younger sister, Cara. Her voice shrilly yelled out words that bounced off the young man's deaf ears. He was a master of ignoring people. Cara knew how to take care of this and proceeded to beat him with her hairbrush until Jason, shielded by his hands, finally grunted loudly and fell out of bed.

"We are leaving in five minutes!" Cara yelled out as she kicked Jason's leg. Her blonde and black dyed hair fell in smooth layers past her ears, and her bangs neatly lay over the top of her head. Makeup adorned her tanned seventeen-year-old face—beautiful blue eyes and glossed lips. All this to complement her thin figure in a skirt and a low-cut white shirt. Yes, she looked like a young woman of the night. I use that phrase because I feel guilty for describing her; perhaps I won't do that anymore.

Jason let loose a soft moan of displeasure, having just been kicked again by Cara before she left the room. We have a twenty-four-year-old lying on his parent's floor, and on top of that he has just been beaten up by his sister. At least the day hadn't started any different.

Jason yawned as he lazily pushed himself up to a standing position. At full slouching height, he stood nearly six feet tall, his body nothing more than a skinny, dark-haired mess.

After stumbling over covers for a minute or two, Jason made his way to a pair of jeans lying on the floor. He proceeded to check them for stenches and stains before pulling them over his red-and-white-striped boxers. After another few misguided steps, he made it to his dresser drawers, where he fumbled through change bins and around a lamp for his keys, only to realize they were already in his pocket along with his wallet.

Another grunt, and he was on his way to the door. He contemplated changing his well-stretched white T-shirt for the colorful polo on the ground, but the threats of his sister rang throughout the house, and he instead followed them.

To his left was a closed door to his sister's room; it always seemed to remain closed. In fact, it was closed so often that Jason wondered how she got in there. *Probably through the window*, he thought.

At this point, Cara was more than likely about to search for an extra set of keys to use to take off in Jason's vehicle. She had wrecked her sports car and lost her driver's license due to a drunk-driving incident. We can call it an incident, but she was fully aware she was drunk. I'm not sure she knew she was driving, however. I'm pretty sure the driver of the car she hit didn't think she was doing much driving either. The other driver probably thought it was more like ramming.

Jason stumbled forward, slowly making better strides as he awoke. Now to his right was the restroom. He quickly leaned his head in to take a peek into the mirror. His face looked about average for him. It was unshaven, with dark-brown hair scattered all over his head reaching as low as his ears.

Just opposite the bathroom a rather large doorway led into the living room. In here sat two couches positioned in an L shape, both with small tables at their ends that supported lamps. Jason guided himself along these until he made it across the room and into the kitchen. Loud chatter could be heard through the glass door exiting the kitchen.

Outside, Cara kept making vibrant hand motions as she chatted away on her cell phone. Jason clumsily stepped over their doormat cat (not a doormat in the shape of a cat, but a cat that acted like a doormat). He then unlocked the doors to his midsize vehicle, a beautiful blue ride with a removable tan roof. Once they both made it into the car, Jason fumbled with his keys for a good minute before starting the engine. He then drove down his parents' driveway.

Large mixes of music blasted from the stereo of Jason's vehicle as Cara kept swapping stations. She hadn't stopped talking on her phone, of course. Jason's mind relished over going back to sleep, and so did his eyes. A few times during the trip, they nearly closed, causing him to rotate the wheel far enough to one side as to have his vehicle travel out of its intended lane. Honks from angry and scared drivers would then awaken him. Strangely, his sister didn't take notice. She was used to being in the wrong lane. I promise I will stop making fun of her accident eventually.

It was not too long before they came to an enormous building. It almost looked as if many buildings had been connected together to form a stretch of buildings. If you haven't had the pleasure of being acquainted with this style of structure, then allow me to introduce you. Reader, this is a mall.

After parking, Cara made her way out of the vehicle and to the nearest entrance of the mall. Jason tiredly lowered his head only to honk the horn on his vehicle's steering wheel; he then quickly looked up as if he were a startled animal. He looked like an animal as well, and I bet he could use a shower. Jason descended from his vehicle. He then walked to another entrance to the mall, different from the one that Cara used.

The mall itself was quite large, with stores all over the place and people everywhere. Some of the people were shopping; others were wasting time. They should know that they are not the only dimension that enjoys such activities. Why, in one dimension it is a way of life to shop each day for what you will wear, eat, drink, and do. Wait ... that is this dimension; forget I said anything.

Jason wandered through the crowds of shoppers, each and every group of people unique to themselves—families, friends, and cultural reference groups, each set as exciting as the next. Oh, look at the young mother pushing a baby stroller. *Whoops!* Jason barely missed running into them. Good thing he apologized.

There was one store in the mall that Jason was interested in, and it just so happened to be Cara's least favorite store—Trendno. It is a store devoted to anti-trendy merchandise. It wasn't the rebellious T-shirts and long pants with chains on them or the hair dye or miscellaneous Gothic-style jewelry that lured Jason to visit this store. No, it was a girl who sat behind the counter that sparked his only interest in being there.

Her name was Sabrina, with her dark-blue shaded hair, too much eyeliner, dark eyes, pale skin, and always wearing a dark outfit of some kind. She was the definition of apathy if it were given a human name and allowed to walk around adorned in dark clothes and makeup.

With a loud thump, Sabrina's hand landed on Jason's back. He looked at her with a half smile as if he should have expected that.

"Hey, what is going on? Toting around that annoying sister of yours again?" Sabrina asked.

"She's not as …" Jason stopped his train of thought after rubbing his back. "Yes, yes I am."

Sabrina made an audible sound of disgust that must have displaced the bright shirt wearing and cheerfully smiling young female who had come up to ask her a question. The sound Sabrina made shook the girl so much that she dropped the silver skull bracelet she was looking at onto the counter and scampered off. Sabrina took notice of the fallen bracelet and grabbed it, stuffing it under the counter. "Just as well. These skulls clash with her smile."

A dark-purple strobe light kept flashing in the far corner of the store. The whole store blinked solely with this color, making it difficult to determine the exact color of some of the merchandise. Black would be a safe bet. Sabrina tilted her head to the side and got behind the counter she was leaning on as an older woman and her son approached the cash register. Her son dressed as if he were trying to look like a vampire—pale flesh, skinny body, and oily black hair. Actually, I think that was just his natural look.

"I don't see why you like these shirts. They look unnatural," the older lady stated. Her face was squished into a look of disgust as she peered over the merchandise the young man had picked out. The young man kept rolling his eyes at each word. It is a surprise that they stayed in his head. She placed a load of shirts onto the counter, her eyes opening wide as if she just realized something.

"A black skull with red eyes? Why can't it be the picture of the man when he was alive?" The lady laughed as she looked at Sabrina, who was preoccupied with scanning the price tags of the shirts.

"I think it represents the darkness of my soul," the young man retorted.

To that, the older lady gave him a joking nudge, which almost sent the young man to the ground. I think she was trying to knock some sense into him.

Jason found interest in the magazine on the counter, one that Sabrina had been thumbing through earlier. It held pictures of miscellaneous pop-culture people of the time. Most of them had red ink over their faces, more than likely done with the red sharpie that lay near the magazine and guided by the hand of a disgruntled Trendno employee.

By now, the woman had stopped poking fun of the young man and opted to pay for the clothes rather than talk him into some brighter summer wear. She handed over her credit card, which Sabrina took and swiped.

Each dimension has a different way of representing one's value and a different method of using it. There is one dimension that figures value as a representation of how many hairs are upon your head. Those with a full head of hair are believed to be the wealthiest and hold places of prestige within their culture. But those who are bald are not bad off either. It is believed that once all hairs are gone, you have reached the pinnacle of society and are dubbed to lead it so others might obtain such success or spending habits. Confusing, I know. Just imagine the process of spending your value; each hair must be plucked from your head, individually. That has to be painful. I'd have little to spend, but much advice to give.

After Sabrina had bagged all of the clothes, she handed the bag over to the lady, who then quickly made for the exit as if she thought the darkness of the store would get to her too. Not to mention the young man was throwing an emotional fit that would cause anyone to become angry with frustration and pity.

Sabrina snatched the magazine from under Jason. She then grabbed hold of the marker and once again returned to her earlier activity. Jason managed another half smile as he watched Sabrina draw devil horns on a famous pop star of the time.

"I don't think red does this guy justice. I'm going to see if we have a black marker." Sabrina squatted down behind the counter, possibly to look for the aforementioned marker. Seconds later, she stood back up; her face had a bewildered look on it. It was as if she knew exactly where she was but was surprised to be there. Within seconds, her eyes met Jason's, who had been staring at a young lady in the store.

Sabrina smiled a wicked smile before hopping the counter. She then curtsied at Jason before running out of the store and into the mall. Jason was confused momentarily; he knew Sabrina hated running. He then started to follow her out of the shop but soon met an opposing force in Cara.

"Figures I'd find you here," Cara stated, steadily pushing buttons on her phone. Her eyes dashed back and forth from the phone to her brother. "The Gs are coming home with us."

The Gs were a group of look-alike girls whom Cara hung out with regularly. They all wore similar clothes and had similar hairstyles. The only remarkable difference from each of them was that they each … wait, there was no difference. Jason tried to look past Cara and see which way Sabrina had run off to, but with each passing moment, his sister seemed to grow larger from impatience.

"Come on dork-a-tor," she apathetically said.

Slight her distinct lack of patience, she was calm in front of the Gs, probably because it was a cool thing to do. The Gs all stood outside of the store; they were playing with their cell phones, periodically looking at Jason. Doesn't it sound silly to say the Gs? Call them friends, call them blood sisters, but why the Gs?

Jason sighed as he reluctantly followed his sister out of the store. On the way out, his foot crunched down on something. After a quick look at the ground, Jason swooped down and picked up the object that he had managed to step on.

In full view of his eyes, hanging between his fingers, was a watch. This wasn't just any regular watch. It had a calculator pad on it, so I guess it really was more of a mini calculator with a wristband attached to it, but then again, the wristband was broken, so it wasn't even that.

After only a moment or two of contemplation on the oddity of finding such an item, and ensuring no one saw him pick it up, Jason pocketed the watch and made his way out of the store and down the long stretch of the mall. The Gs—I have to use that word to simplify things, so give me a break—walked not very far ahead of him. They kept eying every hunky man, clothing store, cute baby, and ample-bodied person in the mall. It was almost if they had rehearsed this display of eye movement because they were in constant sync.

Sabrina was nowhere to be seen, and Jason wasn't too worried. It wasn't her style to be spontaneous, but she did tend to do her most strange activities when she was feeling emotional. Jason just hoped it wouldn't put a damper on her career at Trendno. After all, she was the best at her job. She wore a face of apathy like no other employee.

Starting to feel awkward that he was following a group of teenage girls, Jason pulled out the calculator watch to play with and keep him busy until the fun drive home. The whole keypad lit up when Jason pressed a key. It looked similar to a phone keypad. It had four rows of keys. The top three rows had numbers, and the bottom row had the zero key in the middle with an equal sign on the right side and a strange symbol on the left. Jason guessed it to be a plus symbol that had worn away. Above the keys sat a little LED screen. It was the width of the calculator watch and barely the height of one of the keys. After examining the watch for a good while, Jason realized he had been lagging behind his sister's pace, so he pocketed the watch once again and tried to catch up.

Outside the mall, there was a bustle of traffic and noise between the car horns and people talking loudly on their phones. It was midday on a Saturday in this town, and the mall was becoming a hot spot. After nearly being run over by a honking vehicle, with the music in it turned up so loud that it was a surprise the driver could concentrate enough to drive, Jason jogged to catch up with his sister and her friends at his vehicle.

The Gs were in the middle of an intricate conversation about handsome male pop stars of the day while at the same time discussing the female ones who were going under. It would be interesting to listen to if you were deaf.

The parking lot was full of other idiots, so it took Jason a bit of time to navigate his way through the packed rows of cars and back on the main road. After a few turns through the parking lot and exiting onto the road, he sat practically parked in traffic. While waiting for traffic to move, he enjoyed four young ladies regularly swapping stories and messing with his stereo system. Jason pulled out the calculator watch again. It was all right for him to do almost anything at this moment. No one in his vehicle was paying him any attention.

After a few minutes examining the watch, he began typing in random numbers, pressing different buttons, and realizing that the symbol he thought earlier to be a plus sign did nothing. In fact, the calculator only took in numbers, drawing a string of integers from the left to the right on the LED screen. The equal sign only erased these figures.

A loud honking noise came from behind Jason, followed by a punch to his right arm.

"What are you doing, Jason? Jeez. And I'm the one without my license," Cara stated from the passenger seat. She had broken conversation long enough with her friends to argue that Jason's inability to pay full attention while waiting for traffic to move far outweighed her inability to not drink and drive. Interesting, I know. Soon enough, Jason had managed to catch his vehicle up with traffic, only to come to a stop and wait for another seemingly endless supply of cars to pass by.

This massive tangle of cars wouldn't make much sense to someone who wasn't from here, because the city wasn't large by any standards. That is, unless, your standards come from Dimension-1982022, a dimension where cities never get bigger than a couple houses due to claustrophobic fears. In that case, this town would seem gigantic in proportions, especially at this intersection where one of the city's main roads crossed another main road.

Again enthralled in the watch, Jason completed inputting a lengthy string of numbers into the calculator. He had filled up the whole LED screen this time. Believing he knew its purpose, Jason then reached down to push the equal sign. If it were anything like before, it would erase the numbers and provide him a clear space to type in again. Boredom has its price to be paid. As his finger neared that parallel set of lines, a wave of immediate curiosity rolled over his brain. He instead moved his finger over to touch the worn away button that reminded him of a faded plus sign.

Unknown to Jason at the time, the fantastic calculator-styled watch that he held in his hands was not a calculator at all. It was a Personal Dimensional Transporter, or PDT. Such items were invented to bypass traditional dimensional travel methods. Those persons who don't own a PDT or don't have the brain capacity to create one instead have to locate Dimensional Travel Points to use for traveling purposes. We'll get more into that later.

Upon pressing the button, Jason's body felt as if it were being pushed through a small opening and then shoved into a space impossible for anyone to fit, but he somehow slid through it before once again feeling normal. The change in feeling had occurred so quickly that Jason merely thought he had a major cramp in his stomach. He jerked the steering wheel, lowered his head, and was immediately tended to by a soft hand placed upon his hairy forearm.

"Is everything all right, Jason?" The voice sounded so familiar, but it quivered in a way that made it impossible to be. Believing his sister was messing around with him, Jason shook his head and grinned.

"What? Yes, everything is super cool." Jason stopped talking as he turned his head to look at his sister. Her eyes showed grave concern, something never seen by him before, and her face was no longer caked with makeup. Everything about her was different from what it had been only a few moments ago. Her hair was no longer multicolored, and her outfit was simple and covered her body well.

Jason jerked his head to the road in front him. Traffic had begun to move, so he pressed on the gas. *Surely, this is just a joke*, Jason thought. *I mean, everything else looks similar. Well, minus that DOWN WITH SOCIETY sticker on my front window. Are they playing a game on me? Wait. What about the Gs, and what is with that music? It sounds like a bunch of garbage cans being banged on to the vocals of some grungy singer while a shrieking wildebeest plays the violin, poorly.*

A quick glance into the rearview mirror might possibly solve Jason's suspicion. Surely those girls couldn't have swapped to a new look in a flash of a second. With a quick hand movement to the rearview mirror … *Wait. Why are my fingernails painted black? Take it one issue at a time, Jason,* he told himself. *Okay, the rearview mirror shows three normal-looking teenagers all dressed in conservative clothing. At least they all look similar, so that hasn't changed.*

Behind the three girls, on the back window, was an assortment of stickers portraying different antisociety musical groups and rebellious ideas. At least three of them had a small caricature of a man peeing on another object—truly classy. Jason took note of each. Some of the band names he recognized from friends' playlists—Sabrina's, in particular. Perhaps she was a part of this?

"Are … are you all right, Brother? We tried not to stay that long." His sister's quivering voice entered his ears again. The girls in the back of his vehicle looked semiconcerned themselves. At this point, Jason must have snapped in his mind, a feat that took a high amount of uncomfortable surroundings to invoke and a sinking feeling inside of his gut to understand things weren't right.

"Ha-ha!" he burst out. *Why does my voice sound so raspy?* "You think you are going to pull another Halloween trick on me, but no! Think again."

As if at once, all of the Gs gasped and covered their mouths in some sort of defense. These troublesome girls would not make a fool of Jason again. I mean it isn't like they haven't done it numerous times before, but this time he was figuratively putting his foot down. He put his foot down literally too—on the breaks. His vehicle came to a quick, screeching stop. Other drivers honked their horns at Jason and came to screeching stops also.

Jason quickly unbuckled his seat belt and opened the vehicle door before stepping into traffic and eventually being hit by a car.

CHAPTER 3

A thin plastic curtain separated Jason's bed from the other patient's bed that sat next to his, but it wasn't enough. The other patient's moans of agony and duress filled the whole room until finally a nurse popped in and gave the man some sedatives.

"All better now." The nurse exasperated as she turned to face Jason. She then walked over to Jason's bedside and checked on the equipment next to his bed. "Feeling any better, Jason?" Her warm voice filled Jason's dreams, and her two friends protruding from her top did too. It almost felt as if he had died and gone to heaven, which he repeatedly said to the nurse. She just chuckled and smiled. She'd probably been told that so many times that she'd lost the patience to respond and was just suppressing rage now.

With a light knock followed by the handle to the room being turned, in came Jason's family—his mother, father, and lovely sister. Cara scowled in Jason's direction as if she had been hurt somehow in his accident. In fact, she had been hurt, unknown to Jason at this exact moment. She wasn't wearing the same shirt she had been wearing in the mall or car; this one covered most of her upper body. It was a tendency of hers to play the good girl when their parents were around. This also meant the absence of the Gs, for the most part.

"This place is too cold. At least there aren't any moving cars in here!" His mother laughed as she looked at the others, as if hoping to get a laugh out of them. She then shuffled over to Jason's side.

Jason's mom could be described in a few words: fit, smart, and outspoken. She was a woman who would be a feminist if it were not for her husband, a man full of information, fit, and reserved.

"He hasn't started walking into the light, has he? 'Cause it might be a car!" Again, his mom busted into a chuckle as she placed her hand on the blonde-headed nurse's arm.

"Um, well …" The nurse responded before smiling, seemingly too tired to form a full sentence.

Cara and Jason's father made their way to the opposite side of the hospital bed from Jason's mother. Jason's father, Phillip, reached out to take hold of Jason's hand but was beaten to it by Cara. She had a similar look of concern for Jason now as she had in the vehicle when she was dressed conservatively.

"Brother, if there was anything I could have done to stop that car, you know I would've, right?" Cara asked as a faint tear appeared in the corner of her eye, matching her quivering mouth.

Jason's face showed only confusion and disbelief because he felt she was still putting on a show. Phillip placed his hands on Cara's shoulders and smiled.

"It is all right, dear; there was nothing you could have done." Phillip reassured Cara. "Motorists these days, they never pay attention to the pedestrian." A moment of silence passed before Jason's dad turned to the nurse. "What is the verdict on Jason, a few broken ribs?"

Jason's mom, Leslie, had begun commenting on the drapes and touching many of the pieces of furniture in the room. It wasn't that she lacked concern for Jason's health. She had already been here when they first brought him in and was probably nervously awaiting the results of the medical tests.

Before the nurse could respond to Phillip's question, a man entered the room, a doctor. He stood a fair height, had a bald head and a clean-shaven face, and was wearing glasses. For clothing, he wore the usual required doctor's garb: scrubs, coat, stethoscope, and clipboard. After a few glances at the pages on the clipboard, he looked up at everyone in the room, who were now all looking at him.

"So, Mr. …" The doctor thumbed through some pages on the clipboard, pressing his lips together. He took an abnormal amount of time to search the documents for Jason's last name. When he finally stopped flipping through pages, he looked at Jason over his glasses. "Davis. You have a few bruises on your side but no broken ribs and a bump on your head. None of it looks to be serious. We will keep an eye on you overnight before letting you go back home." Again, he thumbed through the papers on the clipboard.

Leslie moved closer to Jason with a great big smile and reached out to give him a hug. Jason made an audible sound of displeasure as her hands touched his bruises. She quickly pulled out of her hug before giving Jason a kiss on the cheek.

Cara leaned down after their mom had stopped hurting Jason with her loving hug, a tearful look in her eyes. "Brother, I am so happy to know that you are fine." She leaned down closer to give him a light hug, her lips next to his ear. "This is good because I'm going to get you back for punching me." She let up the slight squeeze of her hug and backed off. After only a second of staring daggers at Jason, she averted her eyes toward the doctor while giving their father a hug. "Thank you, Doctor, for everything you've done."

Jason would have scoffed at the display of affection from his sister had he not been wondering at what point in time, if ever, he had punched her.

"Well, good to hear, Doctor." Their father patted Cara on the head before motioning his wife over, making his way to the door. "How about we get some ice cream to ease these rattled nerves?" Phillip made the statement toward Cara, who kept up her concerned facade rather well as she nodded.

The doctor looked first at Phillip and then to the nurse, who had found a chair and was massaging her feet. Again, the doctor thumbed through a few pages on his clipboard before opening his mouth. "Well, we do have ice cream here."

Jason couldn't hold it in anymore. Those eyes, those lips, and that shirt; it all was a show. He then pointed a finger at Cara. "I see you! Yes, you right there!"

Cara had already started to follow their father out the door before she turned to see the finger pointing in her direction. She put on her best confused face as she looked at Jason.

"Now you can't just pull a trick like that off in the car and not expect something to happen!" Apparently, he spoke louder than intended, because more people looked at him than Cara. Then again, he practically had to yell across the room for her to hear. All in all, this was a poor idea on his part.

After everyone stood silent for a few moments, the doctor offered his insight on the outburst. "The slight head trauma Jason suffered can cause delusions. It isn't anything to worry about." Again, he needlessly shuffled through his clipboard. After doing so, he looked up over his glasses to see no one had made a response; they all stood still, as if paralyzed. "Well, all right. If you need anything, ask." The doctor looked around the room before trailing off and inching his way behind the shocked family.

Finally, Jason's mom burst into a chuckle. "Wow! Did you see that? We totally freaked out the doctor!" She looked at everyone with a broad grin. "Okay, come on! Ice cream! Love you, Jason!" She reached her arms out toward Cara and Phillip, pushing them out the door.

Cara gave a stone-cold glare to Jason, wrapped in a vengeful grin. Jason didn't want this gift, but he had to accept it, unwrap it, and play with it a little in his mind. This could only mean trouble later.

After his parents and sister had left, a feeling of brash misunderstanding filled Jason to the brim. Maybe that whole vehicle event was in his imagination?

By this point, Jason realized it was dark outside. What day was it? He could have sworn his mother said something about it. If only there were a calendar on the wall. The room was quite bland, actually—four beds, a few cabinets, ugly plastic curtains, that hiding nurse, and a few posters showing poor children being stuck by needles. Was he in the Pediatric Ward? I bet his parents never swapped over his doctor when he turned eighteen.

The nurse stood up from her hiding spot in the corner. With a yawn, she closed the blinds, squandering Jason's connection to the outside world. She then checked on the other patient before walking to the door and leaving.

Minutes turned into seconds, then into hours, and finally back into minutes where they belonged in the first place. Jason felt bored, and he was hungry for some ice cream. Things weren't going well.

Eventually, he remembered the calculator watch that had been on his wrist and realized it was no longer there.

He started to search through what he was wearing before realizing he was now in a hospital gown, which explained the draft. The watch wasn't on his other wrist either. Hey, don't laugh. That could be a logical place for it to have gone. Finally, he located the watch on a wooden stand next to his bed, as if it had followed him there. It didn't, just so you know. The nurse put it there after having played with it a bit herself.

He picked up the watch and examined it. The LED screen was blank, and the band was broken the same as it had been when he first picked it up at the mall. Just holding it sparked all the memories from before, the strange feelings of delusion and confusion. What was it all about? He was feeling it again. What was going on? Nope, it was just intestinal cramps. Jason slowly slid off the bed and onto his feet. His side ached, and his head felt unstable. He guided himself to the restroom.

After indulging in hospital reading for nearly ten minutes and fighting a losing battle with the toilet paper dispenser, Jason left the bathroom. A familiar sight came across his gaze. A womanly figure stood next to his bed, her back facing him. As he got closer to the woman, he was sure he knew who she was; the mumbling gave it away.

"Sabrina!"

The girl turned around abruptly, rearing a metal box with blinking lights above her head. As she did, it made an awful beeping sound not too unlike a metal detector that has found a prized item below a sandy beach.

The startled look on her face quickly changed to a grin as she saw Jason. She then took notice of the obnoxious blinking box and immediately held it in front of her. The beep grew louder still, causing the sedated patient in the room to start a moaning uproar. Jason looked puzzled and offended. It wasn't because Sabrina had practically broken into his hospital room but because she had reached down and grasped his hand extremely hard.

"I mean, I guess we can hold hands," Jason quenched out as Sabrina's grip became tighter.

Sabrina tossed the metal box over her shoulder to a crashing symphony and started prying open Jason's hand. Within it was the calculator watch, which she snatched up rather quickly. With a cackle, she held it up in front of her, her eyes setting upon it as if meeting its gaze.

"Well, I guess if you really want it … It is kind of cool," Jason stated before sitting down on the bed, feeling light-headed from standing. He noticed something about Sabrina. She had a dark, sinister style about her, and not the good kind. Instead, it was the I-am-going-to-beat-you-with-a-bat-in-your-sleep-tonight-and-then-take-a-picture-of-myself-sitting-on-top-of-you kind. This was different from her typical moody look.

It took quite some time before Sabrina settled down, tears of joy rolling down her cheeks. She looked at Jason, who had once again laid down on the hospital bed.

"You don't realize what this is, do you?" Sabrina's voice took on a new sinister tone, matching her look.

Also, imagine if you will the camera panning in on her face. It sets the mood.

"No," Jason stated as he kept trying to get into a comfortable position.

"This … this here is my ticket away from here. *My* ticket back home, now that I have obtained one of the prized treasures of your dimension!" If lightning struck at any point during that statement of hers, it would have been perfect.

"What prized treasure?" Jason asked. He was used to Sabrina being weird. Often enough, she'd show up at his parents' house at two in the morning to go out and eat. She'd usually just order coffee and complain about her workday or stepdad. Actually, it was a healthy mix of the two.

Sabrina scoffed as if in disappointment and then held up what looked to be an ink pen. "This!" Proudly displaying the ink pen, she placed her other hand on her hip, striking a pose. The pen was in the shape of the Statue of Liberty. The tip of the pen came out of the bottom of the statue, once the base was removed. Jason pushed himself up to get a better look.

"In no way will you foil my plans, again," Sabrina said as she shoved Jason back down rather roughly. She then furiously typed numbers into the calculator watch, keeping up a pretty consistent laugh all the while.

The quick movement that was enforced by Sabrina's hand disrupted Jason's innards, causing him to feel a prominent amount of pain and sickness at the same time. This disruption also disoriented his senses, and within seconds, he had fallen out of the bed and landed on Sabrina's feet. He then wrapped one of his arms around her ankle, trying to use her to help himself up. She was too busy cackling to take notice.

As if he weren't already feeling enough discomfort, his body started to feel wretched and contracted. It only lasted a second in time but felt much longer. Jason wasn't quite sure what happened to him at that moment, but what happened next was expected—vomit. Where at? That place would be all over Sabrina's leather footwear.

Sabrina moved to the side after Jason vomited on her boots. *Was she wearing those before?* Jason was unsure and feeling quite unwell. Sabrina too seemed quite confused and unsure about their current situation.

The wooden door just behind Sabrina opened with a large swing, and in entered a woman dressed in a white blouse, a gray skirt with a white apron over it, and a white nurse's cap. She looked like a nurse from the Middle Ages. She carried a pitcher of water on a plate. Upon looking over and seeing Sabrina with Jason on the floor, she made a loud sound of displeasure.

"What are you doing? This is not how you visit your injured friends!" The young lady quickly brushed past the befuddled Sabrina, who had taken to mumbling to herself, and placed what was in her hands on the wooden end table next to Jason's bed. She then assisted Jason back onto his bed. She was remarkably strong for her size. Perhaps she was used to lifting patients who had fallen from their beds, or perhaps she was a body builder. The clothes she wore left much to the imagination.

The nurse looked worriedly at Jason, whose stomach pains were so great that he kept his eyes half closed. After a few moments, he opened them.

Imagine at this moment that you have just woken up, and you see a light that seems is blinding. The aforementioned light then becomes more tolerable as your eyes adjust to it. Kind of like seeing an angel … well, unless you are in Dimension-1223 … 4 … 5? Oh, I forget. Just acknowledge that there is a dimension where angels are a familiar, blinding sight. Anyway, my point was to say that this is how Jason felt at that moment.

Once Jason's eyes fully opened, they came to notice something rather peculiar about this woman, aside from her clothes. She looked oddly similar to the large-breasted nurse wearing hospital scrubs who was looking after him earlier. The odd clothes and ragged hair of this woman also gave away that she wasn't exactly who he thought she was, but her body spoke differently. What if he told the same pickup line as earlier?

"Have I died and gone to heaven?" Jason asked before forming his mouth into a sheepish smile. He swore he could hear Sabrina's eyes roll. The nurse giggled and blushed.

"No, sir, but I fear your head trauma might have made you overly sweet." The young lady picked up the pitcher and plate. Jason reached out his hand, signifying that he wanted the nurse to wait.

"Wait. How did I suffer this injury?" he asked, having just realized the injuries to his side and head didn't feel nearly as painful as before when he wasn't seeing medieval people. What was painful was his voice. Had he gone medieval also?

"Young sir thought it would be fun to dance in the lane where the carts roll." The woman smiled before walking to the other side of a cloth partition that separated Jason's bed from the patient next to him. He could hear her soft voice whisper words to the patient, words of encouragement.

The room had obviously changed, but maybe it was just in his head. Maybe he had hit it when he fell to the floor; regardless, things were good. *So the walls are covered with tapestries, and there are candles on sticks. At least it is still dark outside, right? Plus Sabrina is back to her mellow self. She is sitting in that wooden chair terribly hard. Contemplating it looks like, very hard.*

After a few moments, Sabrina looked at Jason. "All right, we, as in you and me, are going to get out of here." Sabrina abruptly got up from her chair and moved to Jason's bedside. Jason caught a full view of her in the candle light. She was dressed particularly medieval, wearing a blue corset, white blouse, and dress.

Right mind, good one. Next I'm sure we'll see a knight, thought Jason.

"What? Why?" Jason stammered back, confused. He had all he needed. There was a beautiful lady to take care of him, a bed that was slightly less comfortable than before, and possible ice cream from his parents when he woke up from this dream.

"Why? Well ..." Sabrina took a moment of silence before responding. "This place is strange, and I would feel some remorse if anything critical happened to you."

"Critical?"

"You know, like death."

A few seconds of silence passed before the door opened up again, and in came two rather burly men and another person who looked like a man of faith. Jason sat up and watched intriguingly. Sabrina took this moment to grab hold of Jason and pull him out of bed. She then struggled to get him to stand without requiring her assistance. The group of men had gone behind the cloth curtain, save one of the men who stood watch outside the curtain. Jason beckoned to him and asked what they were doing.

"What are they doing?"

"Why, giving him a lobotomy, sir," the man replied.

Jason looked confused but could see the outline of the preacher person wielding a saw. The patient on the bed seemed to be voicing his displeasure for this enough to make it look like a true lobotomy. Not to mention the fact that they had restrained the man.

"But ... but what for?" Jason asked.

Sabrina had begun trying to pull him toward the door.

"Oh. Says he sees things and that this place he is in isn't where he is from." The young man whispered to Jason as if it'd get him in trouble to say what he just said. "Like some sort of sorcery transported him here from another place. Ha! Crazy man, he is; the priest will fix that though."

Jason's eyes grew in size, and his mind shot out the door, soon followed by his body, and then Sabrina. "What did you do?!" he yelled over at Sabrina. Or was this even the one he knew? Could it be an evil twin? She didn't have a goatee.

The hallways in the hospital, albeit not prior seen by Jason, didn't look like any hospital hallways he'd seen before. They held similar tapestries to the ones in the room they just ran out of and had stone floors. What was going on here? On a closer look at a few of the tapestries, Jason saw they were just ads for different types of medication and surgeries. One had the face of a person stitched on it with his hand next to his head and thumb up while another hand held up a saw. Below it, it read LOBOTOMIES, THE ONLY CURE FOR THE CRAZIES!

Jason soon found himself outside of the hospital with Sabrina, breathing heavily. He kept trying to make a comment on how confused he was about what was going on, but he was sucking in too much air to talk. All the while, his eyes shifted between candles on posts, a carriage, horses, and men clad in armor. *Oh look … knights. What is going on? The layout … it looks so much like …*

Wait a second. Jason thought. Jason stumbled around, looking for a sign, and soon saw one. There was a giant wooden billboard held high above the hospital by a long post. Written across it were the words: ST. JUDE'S HOSPITAL AND ALMSHOUSE. *All right. Where is she?* Jason thought. He turned around and saw Sabrina standing on the steps leading up to the hospital. She was looking at the watch, which was wrapped around her wrist.

Jason moved over to where Sabrina stood and wanted to start a massive scene but instead sat on a step slightly above her, trying to stop his spinning head. He wasn't sure whether the cause of the light-headed feeling was from his injuries or the radical changes in the world around him.

Sabrina kept mumbling many different things to herself. It wasn't until she stated, "… not where I thought I was going …" that Jason stopped her mumbling with a slap on her back. Sabrina turned to face him, her eyes penetrating through him much as Cara's did.

"Tell me what is going on!" Jason couldn't accurately control his voice now. He spent most of his life being a calm person in a busy world, but now that he was freaked out, there was no calmness. Sabrina's expression changed from anger to a broad grin.

"You look hungry." Sabrina reached out and grabbed Jason's arm, half dragging him down the steps and toward the street.

"Wait … what?" Jason fought her pull at first but eventually gave up because he was quite hungry. He followed her lead to a cobblestone street that ran parallel to the hospital building. Far down the path from where they stood, a horse-drawn carriage approached. Sabrina waved her arms at the carriage, then whistled, and showed a little leg. She laughed and nudged Jason as if trying to get him involved.

Once the carriage had come to a stop in front of Sabrina, who was still making motions at the carriage driver, she and Jason both entered it through the door on its side. From the front of the wagon, a tan-skinned man wearing a turban poked his head through a square opening in the carriage.

"Where to?" he asked in a rather perky voice for someone who was up at this hour.

"Somewhere we can grab a good bite to eat," Sabrina replied.

The man nodded knowingly. Apparently, he too had these late night cravings. With a snap of the wrist, the whip in his hand lashed forward, and the horse drawing the carriage started to move.

The inside of the carriage featured little other than the seat they sat upon and another seat in front of them that faced their direction. Jason could see the faint outline of beads coming from around the driver's seat. Was there a light on the top of the carriage? Jason leaned his head out the door and saw a sign written in a medieval type font on the top of the carriage. It had a candle sitting on either side of it that lit up writing that read TAXI.

Sabrina continued messing with the watch whilst Jason finished exploring the inside of the carriage. The driver of the carriage lifted his head toward the two and glanced briefly back at them. He noticed the gown that Jason was wearing.

"Coming from the hospital? Oh ho! Looks like I have a crazy one with me. What were you there for?" The man asked.

"My friend here was dancing gaily in the rain when he decided to run headfirst into a cart. Nothing serious." Sabrina answered the man with a big grin. She looked to be having fun with the current situation. Jason, on the other hand, was not. He made sure she knew it with a deep, concentrated stare. The man turned his head to face forward, apparently stifling a chuckle. Jason couldn't take it anymore.

"It was a car! A car hit me. Because I was disoriented and wasn't sure what was going on," Jason spouted out. He was at wits end and could have sworn one of his eyelids just twitched. Sabrina had a field day with her laughter and even fell to the side.

"A car? Oh pray, tell me what that is?" the man at the front asked, now laughing too. He looked back at Jason and saw a face of pure dislike and then quickly shut up.

Not long after Sabrina had quit laughing, the carriage came to a stop. Out of the window, Jason saw a well-lit store with a sign in the front that read: TACO TOLL. Jason caught the reference; he wasn't amused. The man in the turban pulled the reins on the horse to make it stop. He then turned his upper body around to face Jason and Sabrina.

"That will be two copper pieces," he stated, holding out his hand.

Sabrina rustled through a pouch that was tied around her waist and handed over a few coins. Jason watched for a moment before contemplating the likelihood of everything returning to normal if he were to smash his head on the street.

"Keep the change," Sabrina said.

The man nodded with a smile and pocketed the money. Sabrina pushed Jason from the carriage, forcing him onto the street and causing him to have to fight to keep his balance. The man at the front of the wagon looked over at Jason.

"Careful, boy; you'll flash the whole neighborhood," he said, followed by a warm, hearty laugh. The man whipped the horse drawing the carriage into a light trot.

Sabrina bit her lower lip in jest and grabbed Jason by the arm, leading him toward the restaurant. Through the wooden door, their nostrils were treated to a mix of spices and the smell of other late-night eaters. The inside of the building itself was relatively quaint and looked similar to a restaurant Jason had been to before. There was a long wooden counter with a man standing behind it, tables and chairs made of wood, and plant holders on top of trash bins.

Sabrina moved up to the counter, tracing her eyes along the tapestries that hung above the cashier. Each tapestry had the names of food that was sold here stitched on them, some with crude pictures. The counter was bare of cash machines; at least something fit right in this whole messed up place.

"All right, I'll have a burrito and two tacos, and he'll have," Sabrina said to the man behind the counter. She then looked over at Jason, who had gone into a disbelief shock. His mouth drooped, his eyes were glazed over, and he breathed in long sighs. "He'll have two tacos. Make it three on second thought and two drinks."

The man behind the counter wrote this on a sheet of parchment and added the total up, taking quite some time and requiring the use of all his fingers. Finally, the cashier finished totaling up the price and told Sabrina what she owed. Sabrina handed over the appropriate amount of coins. After the clerk had finished placing the coins in assorted buckets labeled for each and gave Sabrina her change, he set an empty wooden tray on the counter with two empty goblets.

Jason grabbed a cup and then moved over to what he gathered was the soda machine. It was a large wooden box with dispensers made of iron, labels on the wood indicating drink types, and a large block of ice that could be chipped into smaller pieces if you needed some with your drink. After dispensing some drink, Jason found a seat. He had forgotten about Sabrina, who was spending an awful long time at the condiment bar. When she finally did plop down across from him, it was with an enormous sigh of relief.

"Fun day, right?" she asked with another big grin.

Jason stared blankly at Sabrina. One of the men behind the counter blew a horn and then announced that Jason and Sabrina's order was ready. Sabrina motioned Jason to stay seated while she went off to grab the food. Jason didn't object to this, because he was still trying to wrap his head around the whole situation. After a few moments of silent contemplation, Jason saw Sabrina had returned to her seat. She looked at him and then down at the tray of food she had brought back with her.

"Where exactly are we?" Jason inquired as Sabrina removed the cloth wrapping from around a taco.

"Taco Toll," Sabrina responded without so much of a second of thought.

Jason figured she was teasing him, so he persisted.

"I get *where* we are, but in *what* time period?" Jason ensured he emphasized what he said. He hoped this would prevent Sabrina from being smart with her response again.

"The present, of course. Is there any other time?"

Jason's emphasis on words didn't help apparently.

"I guess there couldn't be any other time …" Jason trailed off as he saw through the window that there were people in white coats walking toward the restaurant. He quickly ducked under the table, Sabrina paying him little attention.

"Careful there, crazy bones. You might bring unwanted attention."

"They are out there! They might want to cut open my head!" Jason whispered from below the table.

Sabrina, who had begun eating her tacos, took a look down at Jason and then over at the watch on her wrist. She stretched her leg toward Jason.

"Grab on." She mumbled between bites of taco. Jason, thinking she had an odd way of comforting people, did so.

Moments passed as Jason sat below the table. The door to the restaurant had opened, and in came the individuals in white clothes. They were looking for someone, perhaps Jason. One of them recognized Sabrina and moved over to her side. He asked if she had seen a young man matching Jason's description.

As Jason sat there, knowing for sure he'd be found, he felt as if he'd been punched in the stomach. The feeling lasted only a moment before the world around him once again looked familiar, and he found himself sitting on the cold floor of a restaurant in his hospital gown.

"What ... the ..." Jason's statement was cut off by the quick jerking of Sabrina's hand, helping him from under the table.

"Better get you back to the hospital!" She grinned.

CHAPTER 4

———— ❖ ————

"I thought you knew what you were doing. You did, after all, grab my ankle," Sabrina argued. Jason soon realized that she wasn't going to take the blame for what had transpired. "Besides, everything is normal now! Eat your taco."

"I fell out of the hospital bed … And this taco is cold," Jason retorted. He had managed to eat some of a taco, but his head and side pain had worsened with the latest strange event.

"Whiny little baby," Sabrina said under her breath.

"I vomited on your shoes," Jason spouted out, having heard what Sabrina said. This outburst gathered the attention of nearby patrons.

"That was kind of gross."

After a few moments of silence, Sabrina engorging in tacos and Jason glaring at her, the restaurant's door opened and let in a chilly breeze that brushed up Jason's hospital gown. Why didn't anyone think it odd that he was in one? Well, maybe they thought it was odd but figured he knew what he was wearing in public. At night, all the crazies come out.

A man stepped into the restaurant, followed by a police officer and the same nurse from the hospital, wearing modern nursing clothes. *Interesting,* thought Jason. He had taken his glare off of Sabrina to watch the trio look around the restaurant.

Jason immediately recognized the man currently recognizing him from the entrance to the restaurant. It was the carriage driver that had given them a ride to this establishment.

Where are your medieval clothes now? Oh, wearing ordinary stuff, that doesn't fool me! Such thoughts bounced in Jason's crazy head.

"There he is!" the driver announced, his finger accusingly pointing at Jason. The police officer moved over to where Jason and Sabrina sat.

"Ma'am, is this the man you are looking for?" the police officer asked the nurse.

The nurse had wandered over toward the restaurant's counter. She turned to face the officer when he asked her about Jason. She then nodded, glancing over at Jason, who now stared at Sabrina. She was telling the policeman that Jason was some lunatic who sat down at her table and started eating her tacos.

The nurse and cab driver led Jason out of the restaurant, while the police officer stayed back and questioned Sabrina. The taxi driver made comments about Jason needing to grow up and to stop messing with people. At this point, Jason didn't care anymore, because he just wanted to lie back down.

When they stepped outside of the restaurant, Jason saw the cab driver's taxi, not a carriage. Jason curled into a fetal position in the back of the cab. The taxi driver drove them to the hospital because he said it was the least he could do for such a beautiful nurse and the crazy guy in the back. When they arrived, they carried Jason half-awake to his room and chained him down to the bed. Only kidding about the chains, but they did keep a better eye on him through the rest of the night and into the next morning when he was released from the hospital. He was returned home with some medication to help with the pain when lying down and a few notes about avoiding standing in traffic.

The next few days passed by without anything stimulating happening, and before Jason knew it, he was waking up to another morning in which sunlight was filling his bedroom. Jason stretched out and checked the clock next to his bedside. It read eleven thirty; he was awake too early. He then rolled over onto his side and shut his eyes extra tight to block out any light. Good moments always end in disruptive squalls started by younger sisters, especially those named Cara.

"You have been nursing this bruised-and-battered thing for two weeks now. You will have to face me sooner or later," Cara stated. Her squalls were always like that, calm and then fierce. She had snuck into the room quietly and then intentionally pushed on Jason's bruised side until he opened his eyes. "Mom and Dad somehow blame this on me, but I will take this blame all out on you." She moved her face so it was almost touching Jason's. Her eyes were a burning oven of hate, not conventional. "And you better get up soon. I need a ride out of here."

A light knock on Jason's bedroom door signaled their mother's entrance into the room. Cara kissed Jason on the nose and smiled. She then left the room with a big smile to their mom.

"She has been asking when you'll be better for some time now. I just don't know why she cracks her knuckles every time she hears an answer. Quite a bad habit, if you ask me. So, sweetie, how are you today?" Leslie moved her way to Jason's bedside and checked his temperature. Once Cara had entirely left the room, she smacked Jason lightly on the head with the back of her hand, "How can you be so lazy?" She took a seat on his bed, pushing his legs away with her rear.

"I'm not lazy. I'm just really comfy," Jason argued, trying to pull the covers up to his chin. His mother shook her head before ripping his comforter off of him and almost off of his bed.

"Oh! Honey, your friend, is here. You know, the really weird dark-haired girl from that creepy store," Leslie said. "You know who I am talking about? What was her name?"

"Sabrina," Sabrina stated from the doorway. She was eating a muffin that was apparently pilfered from Leslie's kitchen. The way she leaned against the door had presence, something Jason hadn't seen before. Come to think of it, almost everything about her seemed different from how he remembered her before she ran away from him at the mall.

"Oh, yes! How can I forget such a lovely name for such a beautiful face?" Jason's mom said as she stood and then walked toward the door with a smile at Sabrina.

Sabrina reached out to Jason's mom as she walked by and shook her hand as if neither of them had met before. Sabrina gave her a grin, as was her new signature move apparently. Jason's mom exited the room. Sabrina then closed the door and laid herself out on the bed beside Jason.

"So should we shake hands too?" Sabrina asked after seeing Jason's dumbstruck look.

"Wait," Jason chuckled. "Good one. You hate touching people's hands."

Sabrina looked serious, more serious than she had ever looked before. So serious that it almost blew Jason's mind. The only thing protecting his brain from exploding was a thick wall of sleep that encrusted it already.

"I'm not from this dimension." Queue the dramatic music as Sabrina stated that with a heavy breath.

Jason grinned and propped himself up on his navy-blue bedsheets.

"Stop smiling like that." She directed.

Jason followed her order only in jest. He'd catch her again with another grin in a second.

"I am serious, and you are dumb," she said after Jason let another grin sweep across his face.

Sabrina looked frustrated. She pulled the calculator watch, minus the wristband, from her pocket.

"Wait. I thought you put a new wristband on that, didn't you?" Jason inquired to an annoyed Sabrina. She looked at him, tilting her head, and then looked back at the watch as she typed in some numbers. She then lifted her leg up toward Jason's chest.

"Grab hold of my ankle," Sabrina commanded.

Jason snorted and folded his arms in front of his chest.

"Fine." Sabrina placed the calculator watch forcefully in Jason's hands, pressing a needle against the watch. "Just hit the faded button then." She grabbed hold of one of Jason's hairy legs; her hand felt cold and firm. Jason willingly pushed the button in an attempt to get her to let go of his leg. She had an iron grip on it.

Again, his world was torn. His body felt pain that it hadn't felt in quite a few days, and his mind became numb for only a moment in time. When Jason's eyes regained focus, he looked around his bedroom. *Wait, did it always look like this?* he thought.

"Psshhh, what is …" Jason stopped midsentence because his voice sounded robotic. "This … this does not compute." *Why did I just say that?*

"He-he he-he he-he he-he. This is too funny," Sabrina replied. She was dressed in what looked like aluminum foil with a silver pot on top of her head. "Watch this." Her robotic voice resounded with an eerie echo into the near-void-of-anything room. She then performed simple robotic dance moves: the moonwalk, arm cranking, head turning, and body turning.

Jason looked around what he thought was his room. It was very plain, no colors on the walls, and it felt like he was lying on foam. The foam material had an imprint for where his body would lay that fit his form precisely. There was a computer in the rear of the room. Its screen had a constant scrolling line of zeros and ones that went across it.

Sabrina removed the watch from Jason's wrist, placing it on hers with slight difficulty. She let out a giggle when Jason tried to assist her with the watch, a giggle that would send chills up the spines of those not used to such voice sounds. From the sight of things, she was enjoying herself too much.

"Okay, I give up. What is going on here?" Jason asked, sitting straight up in his bed now and moving stiffly from side to side. No matter how hard he tried to will himself to, he couldn't get himself to move like a regular human.

"Having trouble getting comfortable?" Sabrina asked with a robotic grin of mostly teeth and no emotion in the eyes. "We are in another dimension. One apparently focused on people acting like robots."

"Di … dimension?" Jason repeated back as he managed to figure out how to move his body in a way to get off of the foam bed and onto the cold floor. He was dressed in what looked like aluminum foil pajamas. *Don't ask*, he thought.

The different outfits they wore crinkled with each stiff movement. Jason enjoyed moving like this. He hadn't had much luck in his own dimension when it came to doing the robot, but here he could perform the moves so seamlessly. *Why was it like this?* He had to ask. As he opened his mouth to spout out the question in a robotic monotone, the door to his room opened, and there stood a shorter figure wearing an aluminum-looking tank top and skirt.

"Cara," Jason stated, almost as if it helped him better comprehend what was going on.

"Yes, it is me," Cara replied. "Now get moving. You are driving me to Eric's house so we can perform complicated equations."

Jason smirked inside because his face wouldn't move the way he wanted as he thought about what equations they could be doing. Maybe they were going to derive the square root of a radical.

He wasn't quite sure why he did it, but instead of following Cara, he started dancing.

"Eric can wait. Sabrina and I are having a party!"

Sabrina laughed robotically as she too performed some robotic dance moves. Namely, the move where you lean forward and let one of your arms dangle, moving it back and forth until you finally stop it. Cara didn't look amused by this and began shuffling toward Jason. He knew there must've been something angry going through her mind: does not compute, destroy, take keys, and then buy a shorter skirt.

Jason wasn't quite sure where the confidence he now possessed came from, but he liked it. He turned his back to Cara and jokingly mooned her, pants on, of course. Cara continued to move toward Jason, but now she had her arms outstretched; the beast within was enraged. This made her look less like a robot and more like a zombie on the hunt for brains. All the same, she grasped Jason's hair, which was matted with hair gel, and reared him around to slap him on the face.

Sabrina, who had been checking on the watch, pushed Cara away with stiff arms and sent her tumbling to the floor. She then looked at Jason. "Grab hold of my ankle, you rebellious robot-man."

Jason had fallen to the floor due to his sister's firm grip on his hair, so he just reached out a hand and grabbed Sabrina's ankle.

Again, the rush of regurgitating feeling came over Jason as his room returned to its usual form. He felt the scene was familiar because he was once again lying in the fetal position on the floor and wearing less clothing than should be worn whilst being looked down upon by a woman who he now believed to be an escaped lunatic. At least he as having fun, and isn't that what escaped lunatics are all about?

Sabrina helped Jason to a sitting position on his bed as he held his stomach. This time the feeling lingered a bit longer than before.

"I forget that you haven't done much dimension traveling. Your body isn't used to it," Sabrina stated as she took a seat next to Jason.

"Dimension this, dimension that! Dimension my cat … I'm not entirely sure why I just said that. Could you please explain what is going on?" Jason asked as he tried to stand up to see if that would make his stomach feel any better. It didn't, so he instead collapsed to the floor.

"Smooth." Sabrina grinned and lay down on Jason's bed. "Dimensions are alternate realities that are only seen once traveled to. For example, we just visited the dimension where people think they are robots."

They both stayed in silence for a minute.

"Okay, all right, that makes perfect sense." Jason finally replied. "We have people on this dimension who do that also." Jason's wits hadn't accepted defeat yet, and he'd do whatever it took to keep them from leaving. This eventually would all make sense, he assured himself. He just needed to cover his ears and pretend he was dreaming.

"Exactly. That is because you live in a Control Dimension." Sabrina sat back up and then noticed Jason's confused look and saw his hands make their way up to his ears. "A Control Dimension is a sort of congregating point for other dimensions." Jason's interest became peaked. "Well, you see … it is like … how about I just show you around some dimensions. Maybe that will help explain things, and you can have some fun."

"You consider my stomach pain and mind confusion to be fun?" Jason asked, having managed to prop himself up against his desk.

Sabrina nodded back without any thought of it.

"I should've known that answer," Jason noted.

"Stop being a sissy." Sabrina got off of Jason's bed and took a few steps to get next to him, sticking out her leg. Jason accepted his fate in not being in control of this situation and latched on to her ankle, whispering desperate words as he sought the aid of any who could hear him. Sabrina was the only one in earshot, and she was too busy grinning and typing into the wristband-less watch.

The next few hours in time involved some gut-punching pain from Jason, as well as travel through multitudes of dimensions. They finally ended up in a dimension of fantasy, literally. The whole landscape looked like a scene from a generic fantasy story where the princess marries a handsome prince and lives happily ever after. Sabrina wasn't keen on waiting too long in this dimension. Actually, she looked rather uncomfortable, but Jason's face had turned pale from all the traveling, so she told him that she'd give him a break.

"You look like you never left the Dress-Like-a-Ghost Dimension," Sabrina stated. She sat down on a well-rounded rock beside Jason. They were in the middle of some enchanted forest where I am sure something magical was happening. "We could have stayed longer too if you hadn't tried to prove that girl wrong about being a ghost. They take it seriously, you know." Sabrina gave Jason a big grin.

"There are a lot of dimensions, aren't there?" Jason asked, color returning to his face. Just then, a dancing rabbit hopped on by, and a group of fireflies in the shape of a heart flew overhead.

"Yes." Spoke the uncomfortable-looking Sabrina as she fidgeted on the rock and checked the watch periodically.

"And which one are you from?" Jason turned his head to face Sabrina as her grin finally started to fade. She turned to face him and opened her mouth but didn't say anything for a moment.

"Took you long enough to ask, but I guess your head is still wrapping around all of this." She reached out to touch Jason's face but stopped just as a shiny butterfly landed on it. Then the most obscure thing happened. It smiled at Sabrina. It had such a beautiful smile that shone so brightly on its little face that the world seemed at peace for a moment in time. Sabrina flicked the butterfly off of Jason's head.

Jason, who had been patient up to this point, became rather agitated at Sabrina and was going to say something rude to her, but he was interrupted by another magical creature of the forest. It was a small limping animal that was making its way through the happy magical forest full of happiness. Small splotches of blood landed on the sunny forest floor as the creature limped nearer. Each stain of blood turned into magic red dust after landing on the ground. The little creature released a whimper for help before collapsing at Jason's feet.

The creature looked very similar to a koala bear with pale fur and dim blue eyes. It limped on two legs and collapsed on its whole body, lying in a mess of hair and big ears at Jason's feet. Sabrina broke a limb from a nearby magical tree, and Jason swore the tree made a sound of displeasure. He reached a comforting hand down to the little creature. His impatience toward Sabrina had fallen by the wayside at the sight of the poor creature in pain. The creature responded with another whimper and a piercing gaze at Jason with those dim blue eyes.

"He looks hurt," Sabrina observed, prodding the creature with the tree branch. Jason's eyes grew as big as the magical, now moaning, creature's eyes as he quickly disarmed Sabrina of the branch.

She looked at him, "He might have rabies or be a witch."

"What makes you think that!? He … he … argh!" Jason's frustration grew again as he kept looking between Sabrina and the little creature who began grasping for Jason's leg, pulling itself to a standing position.

"Anything and all that we have seen today has not put your mind into a state of semialert? I mean, the pumpkin man and his buddies from the Vegetable Dimension were about to eat you." Sabrina argued as her eyes darted to the calculator watch on her wrist. She looked to be getting antsy.

"Okay now. The pumpkin guy was trying to give me a hug. I mean, if anything, he should have eaten you for suggesting that he jump in the hot pools so you could steam him and then make a pumpkin pie." Jason had forgotten the creature for a moment. It was now standing at its full height of a foot and a half, tugging on his pants leg.

"Oh no. You said you were hungry and I was just trying to score us a free, and possibly delicious, pie." Sabrina retorted, having crossed her arms and now looking out into the very magical forest.

"Me ..." a strained and relatively high-pitched voice stated.

"Yes, you. You said you were hungry," Sabrina reiterated.

"M ... me ..." Again the voice sounded.

"Okay, the whiny voice isn't working and is rather pathetic." Sabrina turned her head to look at Jason, but he wasn't looking at her. Instead, he had the little bear creature in his lap. It kept making feeble cries as Jason searched for a wound. "Getting friendly with it now. Great."

After a few moments of searching, Jason located a small splinter in its paw. Finding this ironic, Jason laughed. "Pull the thorn from the lion's paw, and he becomes a cuddly cat."

Sabrina looked closer, as if she were interested in knowing what he was talking about. "Well, he is already cuddly. I bet he turns into a grizzly bear and eats you," she noted.

Jason shrugged off the unprovoked attack against his natural kindness. He then delicately used two of his fingers to slowly remove the sizeable thorn from the small critter.

After a few moments of tossing back and forth in a fit of duress, the creature finally squirmed to a sitting position. Its once pale-blue eyes had changed shades to a dark blue that shone brightly with kindness—the kind of compassion that makes people like Sabrina sick, people who are currently dressed in a white puffy princess dress while sitting next to a man dressed like a prince. If you can't guess, all the dancing creatures and butterflies were for these two. They interrupted their own wedding. It involved Sabrina laughing, Jason vomiting on the doe holding their rings, and then a mad dash to this rock.

"Okay, I might have been inconsiderate," Sabrina admitted after a few moments of silence. She looked over at Jason and the bear. Both were now playing patty-cake together. "Stop trying to be cute." Jason looked at Sabrina with a half smile. "Not you, dumb-dumb," she noted, "the bear. Don't get a big head, but I have enjoyed these last few hours." Jason's smile became full-fledged, which made Sabrina scoff and push him and the bear off of the smooth-surfaced rock.

With a thud, Jason landed onto the magical and possibly enchanted floor of the forest. The koala-looking bear fell not too far from him and let out another call of distress, which made Sabrina roll her eyes again.

"It is just that … ugh, what a stupid dress!" Sabrina acted as if to tear the dress off but stopped when a relatively portly fairy flew toward her face. The fairy couldn't have been more than a foot tall, perhaps three inches around the midsection, with a blue glow and sparkles falling from her wings that never touched the ground but vanished from sight instead.

By this time, Jason had gotten up and was once again sitting on the rock. He made a face at the fairy that showed bewilderment. The little bear made a face at Sabrina that showed heartbreak for being pushed.

"I toil away to give you the perfect wedding like you wanted, and how do you repay me? You beat a couple of birds with your flowers and kick a squirrel!" The fairy yelled out, grabbing Sabrina by the hair and pulling her forcefully closer. What she said was true in all shapes and forms, but she did leave out Jason throwing up on a doe. "And then your future prince vomits all over one of the most beautiful creatures of this forest!" Never mind, she didn't.

The fairy propped herself up against a tree and magically produced a cigarette that magically lit. She took a few puffs that formed different shapes of creatures, each one with angry eyes aimed at Jason and Sabrina. The fairy then took notice of the blood-stained fur on the bear sitting on Jason's lap, and her eyes narrowed further than one could imagine.

"And you are still hurting creatures?!" The once lovely blue sparkles became red fireworks as the fairy made her way over to the bear, but she immediately calmed down upon looking into its profound blue eyes. She then reached a hand out to pet it lightly, looking over at Jason as she did so. Jason had taken a defensive stance, similar to the one he took when his sister prepared to beat him with her hairbrush. Through the space between his defensive wall of arms, Jason peered out at the fairy who had returned to the tree she was leaning up against earlier.

"Uh … you're not going to hit me. Right?" Jason asked as he started to let down his arms.

"What? Oh no, he's playing you on that wound." The fairy answered back. She seemed to have calmed down quite a bit by this point and began pacing back and forth on the ground. I know, she has wings, but she chose to walk.

Sabrina looked at the watch on her wrist, and a grin formed across her face.

"What? I saw blood." Jason stated, searching the bear's fur and pointing to the stain. He then looked at the forest floor, but he could not find the splatter.

"He's a Drama Bear. They do that." The fairy noticed Jason's confused look. "Magical forest, talking does, dancing rabbits … why shouldn't the bear in your lap like to perform drama? Mindless youth, sometimes I wish I was a school counselor." The fairy took a significant drag on her cigarette.

"Fascinating. Jason, would you mind grabbing on?" Sabrina turned her body, setting both of her legs over the bear on Jason's lap. Jason grabbed a leg with one hand.

"Ah, I see that watch. You are Dimension Jumpers. You'll get caught one day!" The fairy yelled out after having taken notice of the leg move and the watch on Sabrina's wrist. "And don't forget that you ruined somebody's wedding!"

Sabrina looked down at the fairy and waved her hand. "I would say fascinating with a sarcastic tone, but I've already done that once, so how about this? I just don't care. And you shouldn't smoke magic dust. It makes you grumpy!"

The fairy's sparkles changed into a dark-red hue again but soon faded from sight as Jason hurdled over in pain.

They now were in the less magical park outside of Jason's neighborhood. Jason recognized this park because it was a place he'd escape to when he was much less mature. I'd say roughly a year ago.

CHAPTER 5

Daylight was dimming through the trees. Both Sabrina and Jason sat on a rock next to each other. A cuddly bear lay resting on Jason's lap. Wait, that can't be good. Sabrina looked over at the bear wrapped around her leg and tried to wiggle it off unsuccessfully.

"Great, maybe we will get caught after all then," Sabrina said, her eyes rolling to the far reaches of her head. The bear looked up at her with its innocent eyes and yawned, showing its pearly white teeth. "Cute." She stated with a significant hint of sarcasm.

Jason noticed he had returned to his normal PJ pants, T-shirt, and boxer-briefs, while Sabrina was dressed in this dimensional personality's Trendno uniform. Things were back to normal once again—sort of. Jason looked over to see Sabrina inputting numbers into the watch.

"No! No more for now. Give me a few days to rest, and we'll go again!" Jason pleaded with Sabrina. It was evident his body was worn out from the many dimensional jumps.

"What are you talking about? We have to return the bear to its dimension. You heard the fairy. We'll get caught." Sabrina argued back, doing her best impersonation of the fairy. She spent awhile pushing buttons on the watch before becoming visibly frustrated and looking at Jason. "You don't remember what I typed, do you?"

"What? How would I know? I thought you knew what you were doing." Jason stated, absentmindedly rubbing the little bear's tummy as it playfully moved its legs and arms back and forth.

Sabrina burst into laughter. "Nah, I just type things in randomly and then use this!" She pulled out what looked to be a needle, the same one Jason had noticed before. The head of it was much more round compared to any typical needle he'd seen before, and it had a series of really tiny bulbs on it. "You see, you stick it against the watch, and it'll let you bypass pesky restrictions and make your dimensional jump more discrete. That is, if you don't bring a bear back with you from another dimension."

Jason was overly intrigued by the needle and reached for it but was swatted away rather quickly by Sabrina while she stood. She then stuffed the needle into a black cylinder, which oddly looked like something one would put a roll of film into, and then put a cap on it before placing it in her pocket.

Jason asked, "Who would be tracking you?"

"I don't exactly know. I've only heard rumors." Sabrina paused for a moment before speaking again. "All right, I'm off for a bit. Going to go and do me some research." She made air quotes with her fingers, her eyes shifting back and forth. She then outstretched a hand to shake Jason's. "Until next time!"

Jason shook it. At least he had sorted out that this wasn't the Sabrina he knew. Speaking of which, where was she?

"But wait … What about the bear?" It was too late. Sabrina had already sprinted off. He could swear he heard her cackle as she ran. In fact, he recalled she would cackle anytime she started running.

Jason sat there deep in thought before finally rubbing his unshaven face and standing. He plopped the bear on his shoulders, so its feet lay on either side of his neck. "All right buddy, you are with me then." The bear made a small sound of agreement and began playing with Jason's messy hair.

It didn't take long to escape the park premises, but along the way Jason noted a few odd sights. For one, he saw a man sternly look at him as the man was trying to dust off a slab of meat, perhaps deer. It looked as if someone had buried it six feet under the ground. Another sight that caught his attention was that of a creepy-looking man leaning against a tree and talking to a police officer. It wouldn't have seemed odd if it weren't for the fact that the man looked as if he were the one filing a complaint, not some poor soul he was stalking. The man talked about a lady who stepped on his foot before complaining that he was ruining her wedding when all he did was bid her a hello.

While walking down the familiar streets to his house, Jason also took note of his lack of shoes. He decided to stick close to the grassy yards. The people whom he passed stared as he walked on by. They were probably staring because of his unshaven face and PJs. That is what he thought, at least. I'm betting the stares had to do with the little bear that kept chewing on Jason's hair and giving wide-eyed stares. I have to admit it is quite a cute thing, but probably really dangerous too.

After passing a multitude of similarly shaped houses with similarly shaped lawns and similarly shaped people gazing at the sight of him and a bear, Jason made it to his parents' home. An extra car sat in the driveway, and his vehicle was still lodged in the garage. *Good*, he thought. Whatever caused him to leave his house in his PJs at least didn't take his car for a spin.

Upon entering the household, he was greeted by his father who was mending a broken frame with tape. He looked over at Jason with a sigh. "Are you all right in the head now?" he questioned. The frame he was working on had a beautiful portrait of a peacock painted by Jason's grandmother in it. The frame was split down the middle, and the bottom portion of it was bent. His father noticed the bear. "Ah, I guess not then."

"What happened?" Jason asked, suspecting it was their visitor, Cara's current boyfriend, Eric. Eric was a careless young man who had ambitions to live the rest of his life on his father's money. Jason wasn't quite sure what the young man's father did for a living, but he was sure it must be significant enough due to the constant trouble the young man got into and the way he always seemed to weasel out of it.

"You did it. Don't you remember? Maybe you did get hurt in that accident more than we all thought. You kept trying to jump through the painting, saying you would love to visit the land of peacocks." Jason's father spoke as if it were just a story he was telling again. He looked at the bear on Jason's shoulders; it waved at him, and he waved back.

"That uh … it must have been the medication," Jason replied, knowing that he was no longer taking any medication for the incident but hoping his father didn't.

"Yeah, must be. I'll get your mom to call and see if they'll change what you are getting to something that keeps you from going insane."

Jason nodded with a fake, toothy smile as he edged past his aggravated father and moved from the front hall into the living area. It was as he thought. The boyfriend was in the building. He sat there with his spiked hair, suave eyewear resting between the spikes, trendy shirt and shorts, and armband tattoo that didn't quite go all the way around his arm. He said that his father wouldn't pay to have the tattoo completed and that he would have to fork over whatever cash he made to get it finished, which was none. I wouldn't doubt the reason he hasn't finished the tattoo is because he can't take the pain.

Cara looked at Jason with a glare of anger. Jason suspected if their mom weren't in the room chattering, Cara would have leaped in for the kill. Jason's mother took notice after his arrival, stood, walked over to him, and then quickly grabbed his arm, practically dragging him over the couch to sit beside her.

"Jason! Nice to see you are home. How was your adventure?" she asked. Jason looked back at her confused, unable to respond before she started talking again. "Oh! What a cute little fellow. Did you take it from the zoo?" His mother laughed, petting the bear.

The bear, upon getting attention from Jason's mother, quickly transferred to her shoulders. Within seconds, it was playing with her short, highlighted hair. It was either looking for bugs or just trying to make it as messy as Jason's. Cara kept setting her glaring eyes upon Jason whenever their mother didn't look her way. Her boyfriend sat rather still, playing with his cell phone.

"I see you broke grandmother's painting," Cara stated, her eyes dim shadows casting a cloud of rain and lightning above Jason's head.

"Oh, dear, he didn't break it. Just rammed into it enough so that it fell, bending the frame and cracking the glass. That is all!" Jason's mother said as she aggressively fought with the bear, trying to stop it from playing with her hair. She finally gave in and looked at Jason with a stressed smile. He obligingly pulled the bear off her shoulders and sat it in his lap. "So, where *did* you get the cute little guy?" She asked, brushing her hair back into place. I imagine that she thought she had fixed her hair back into place, but the truth be told, it was too far out of place to go back without a hair stylist.

"Umm …" Jason stalled for time, realizing nothing he had currently in his head would make any sense to them, so he figured he'd just tell a lie. "My head is hurting. Let me lie down for a bit, and we'll talk later." He stood up and once again placed the bear on his shoulders. He then walked to the end of the living room and rounded the corner toward his bedroom, ducking to ensure the bear didn't hit its head on the door frame.

"Oh. Well, okay, honey. Leave me here with these lively two. I'll bring some cat food for the bear and check on you later." Leslie said, still messing with her hair. "Oh, and I left my powder on your bed."

Cara looked confusingly at their mom. Her boyfriend looked as well, having stopped typing on his cell phone.

"Do what now? Why would I need your powder on my bed?" Jason asked, quickly returning to view. He placed a hand on one of his hips, seemingly negotiating in the air with his other hand.

"I'm not quite sure. You told me it was an emergency and stated that I needed to put on more. You aren't into this Goth phase, are you?" It was too late. Her voice trailed around the corner into Jason's bedroom only to be drowned out by the slamming of his door.

Inside his room of solitude, aside a few things being knocked over, it was in order. Oh, and a painting of an incredibly cool-looking battle hero had found its way to his floor, maybe a connection to his grandmother's art? In fact, it was a connection. Not long after going to the Do-the-Robot Dimension, they went to the Painting-Travelers Dimension. The dimension is so named because people within it can travel into paintings and explore more than the artist created. It is even possible to move between paintings if the paintings are close enough together. As for the powder, it would seem that one of Jason's alter-dimensional personalities who had come here wanted to look more like a ghost.

Jason plopped down on his bed with the bear on his belly. His eyes wavered between opening and closing. The day had been quite a tiresome test of aggravation and confusion. He figured sleep would be the best medicine. Surely in a few days, Sabrina would return to explain things. Yeah, that will happen.

Within moments, he had fallen asleep. His dreams danced before him like waves of dancing magical rabbits. They moved quickly and did not make sense. It wasn't until his room became more humid and experienced a temperature change that he awoke into the darkness of the night. Not too far from his bed he heard a crunching sound, continuous and loud. Jason was not sure what it was, so he looked over the side of his bed and saw the little bear with a bowl in its lap. It was taking handfuls of the cat chowder Leslie had gathered for it and stuffing them into its mouth. A bowl of water was not too far from the bear. It casually took a sip of the water while Jason watched and then gave him a big toothy smile before returning to the food. Jason worriedly smiled back, not sure what to think of that sight. He then lay back down as he was before. He was a little uncomfortable lying on his back, so he decided to turn to his left side.

"Ah!" Jason yelled out as he backed off his bed, falling to the floor and scattering the little bear creature and its food and water. A familiar face peered over his bed, looking down at him. It was Sabrina. She had crawled in through his window, which had apparently been opened by someone on this side. Maybe it was done by a certain magical bear?

"What? How'd you get in here?" Jason muttered.

"The bear let me in. Nice little fellow" Sabrina replied.

What did I tell you? Jason glanced over at the bear. It was eating the pieces of food that had been scattered all over the floor.

"So, I think I figured it out!" Sabrina announced, holding the calculator watch in front of her and putting the pin against the side of it.

"That didn't take long," Jason stated as he pushed himself up to a sitting position. "And how do you know where I live?"

"I saw your address on the clipboard back at the hospital, and when does it ever take me long?" Sabrina retorted with her usual humongous grin. She then spoke before Jason could respond. "Don't answer that, not even in your head. I can hear your thoughts."

"What? No, you can't!" Jason spat out, having stopped momentarily from gathering up the cat chow that was spread out on his bedroom floor.

"You know I'm not from this dimension, and that is all you know! So shut up and let me do my thing." Sabrina began typing into the calculator watch once again. Her eyes opened wide as she cackled. "I've done it." Little lights lit up on the small pin she had put against the side of the calculator watch. She then rather quickly lifted her left leg out toward Jason. He noticed she had cut the bottom half of her pants off, and Sabrina took notice of him taking notice. "What? I was hot. Grab hold already!"

Jason reached his hands out obediently and took hold of her ankle, assisting the bear in doing so also. He realized all the implications and problems that had occurred from doing this the past few times, but between his sister's cold, dead stare and his mother's questions, he needed to get away. Also, there was the whole matter of returning the bear.

Sabrina cackled as she pressed the button on the calculator watch. Maybe Jason had finally gotten used to dimensional traveling, maybe he was thinking too much to notice, but when the world once again shifted around him, he felt no gut-retching pain.

Jason looked at his surroundings and found this to be the oddest of places. They all three sat on a dark-wood floor that felt neither cold nor hot. Around them was absolute darkness, save for a lit lamp that was held up by a long, metal, grooved pole with a square base. It sat dead center in the square room that they were in, and they were positioned in the far corner. Was it the south, east, west, or north corner? Jason wasn't sure of that, but I am sure that it is the least of his concerns right now.

The room was fenced in with an iron picket fence that had small, triangular points on the top of each post. Jason saw a sparkle of light in the distant darkness past the fence and then another just a few inches from the first. Were these stars? The white light from the lamp illuminated only the room, so anything could be out there. Jason noticed just opposite from where they all gazed was a set of stairs that seemed to head upward to nowhere from here. The only thing he could tell is that they angled to the right after only what looked like half a dozen steps up.

Jason stood up while placing the bear on his shoulders. He then reached down a hand for Sabrina. He noticed he still wore his nightwear, while she was dressed in overalls and a T-shirt that had what looked like black powder stains on it. No need to worry; he was moving onward now. Was this courage? Or the spirit of adventure? I personally think Jason was tired of sitting there because it was hurting his rump.

Sabrina took his hand, using it to help herself up. After standing, she crossed her arms in front of her chest, looking around with wide eyes.

Jason thought she looked concerned. "Is everything all right?" he asked.

"It … I don't know. I hope so," Sabrina responded, her voice wavering.

Jason smiled. He felt odd being the one who wasn't at odds with the current dimension that they had traveled to. He then walked over to the railing opposite the stairs. The stars he saw weren't just parallel to them but rather under and above as well. There were far too many even to dream of counting them all. Jason tried to form constellations with them, but he couldn't remember how they should look or if these stars were the same as he saw in the night sky.

Jason also wasn't sure if the platform they stood on was moving. It seemed like the platform was suspended in space. He felt no wind brushing past him, but he did notice that he could breathe just fine. All in all, he wasn't getting far playing the detective. He should have just asked Sabrina. I'm sure she knew all along where they were. It was a place people from her dimension had heard about and feared.

Upon turning around, he could see that Sabrina had moved to lean against the lamppost. She kept her head lowered, as if ashamed of something. Jason looked up to where the stairs led and noticed how, very much like the rest of the dimension, it was odd. The reason it was odd was because he couldn't see past the first turn of the steps. It was as if they vanished into the darkness.

"Well, this certainly isn't a forest. You don't see any of your friends, do you, little guy?" Jason asked the bear on his shoulders, not really expecting a response, which was good because he received none. He then walked to Sabrina's side, having seen enough of the emptiness. Once there, he placed a hand on her folded arms. She looked up at him. "Shall we try the stairs?" he asked.

Sabrina nodded at Jason, her face a nervous wreck.

Jason led her to the stairs, took a deep breath, and began climbing them.

Chapter 6

At the top of the stairs, Jason noticed a few things. There were no walls, but rather fencing surrounded the whole area. The fencing looked the same as the fencing on the floor below. A door sat between fencing on one of the walls and seemed to open into nothing. The stars still twinkled in the sky, and the only thing that lit up this room was a television with a rather large screen facing a couch. The television screen kept swapping between different scenes of people, places, and things. It was as if someone were flipping through the channels, trying to find something good to watch.

Over the top of the couch, Jason saw a head covered with light-brown hair. He approached the couch from the side, practically dragging Sabrina behind him. As he peered over the side, he saw a younger fellow sitting there. The younger guy was dressed in jeans, a T-shirt, and shoes. The young man held a slender device in his hand with a single button on it.

"Excuse me, where are we?" Jason asked, his eyes shifting between the television and the young man. Eventually, the young man looked over at Jason with a look of boredom. He then turned his head to face over the couch toward the closed door.

"Dad, you've got visitors!" the boy yelled out toward the door. He then looked over at Sabrina for a second before returning to the television.

After waiting a few minutes, in which Sabrina kept mumbling things under her breath while trying to use the watch, Jason got tired of nothing happening, so he left Sabrina with the young man and headed over to the closed door. Jason idled at the door for a moment and took a deep breath. The bear gave him a reassuring pat on the top of his head.

The door handle of the dark wooden door was made of similar iron to the fencing that surrounded this room. He turned it gently, pushing the door inward. It revealed another room, which Jason was surprised to see. He took a moment to look at the door frame and even reach past it to the other side of the door before accepting its strangeness.

Inside the room, an older man sat in a recliner, his feet propped up, and head laid back. From the distance he was from Jason, he looked to be snoozing. Jason quietly entered the room, getting a better look at the man. On his head and covering most of his face was a gray bowler cap. He also wore a white button-up shirt, tie, and slacks but currently no shoes, only socks.

He was snoring rather loudly, filling the room with his noise. This room didn't fully match the others. It was actually enclosed by four walls and had a ceiling to it, although the walls and ceiling were still a dark color. The room was full of an assortment of knickknacks and neat piles of clothes. Jason peered around the room and saw some photos on a shelf. They were pictures of random female celebrities. *How odd*, he thought.

While better examining the photos and recognizing quite a few, the snoring stopped, and Jason heard the chair creak. The man had stood up and was looking over at Jason, rubbing his eyes all the while. He put on some nearby slippers and walked over toward Jason, who had picked up one of the pictures.

"It is a lonely job up here, and a guy needs some attention." The man put his hand on Jason's uncomfortable shoulder. "I'm just messing with you! Those are my son's, the lazy oaf on the couch. Yes, I heard him call my name. I was just trying to psych out the young girl you are with." With that, he chuckled and gave Jason a hearty pat on the back. He stood near in height to Jason, who noticed the gray-and-black hair coming out from under the man's bowler cap. "Come now and let us see what caused you to arrive here!" The man led Jason out of the room and toward the couch.

Sabrina was now sitting beside the young man who kept trying to get his arm around her shoulders, but she just brushed it off each time and repositioned herself farther away from him. She then looked over and saw Jason and the other man leave the room Jason had entered earlier. She quickly stood up and walked toward them.

"I see you have become well acquainted with my son." The man commented upon seeing Sabrina. The bear on Jason's shoulders reached over and grabbed the man's bowler hat, pulling it off and revealing his bald head. The man promptly took it back, placing the bowler hat firmly on his head before moving toward the couch and giving the bear a small smile.

The younger man had sprawled out on the sofa by this point, probably emotionally hurt from one of Sabrina's sharp rejections. His father sat down on the couch, pushing the young man's feet aside. He then picked up the device his son was using earlier from off of the floor and glanced momentarily at Jason. "Come, take a seat."

The young man tried to motion Sabrina over next to him, but she opted to stand instead. Jason took the open seat between the father and son. After the man had taken control of the device, we'll call it a remote from now on, the screen that once showed the random images the son was watching instead showed that of a forest. A very magical forest that looked familiar to Jason.

"See, here is where you two messed up. You ticked off the fairy." The man used the remote to zoom in on a section of the forest, which showed a replay of their events from the Fantasy Dimension. It showed the fairy magically create a cigarette while the cuddly bear Jason was tending to was midswing in its drama act. "So, what did you name him?" the man asked, motioning to the bear.

"Um ..." Jason stalled.

"How rude of me," the man said. "We haven't had any introductions! My name is Jonas, and this is my son, Trandon." Jason looked at Sabrina, expecting to exchange smiles after hearing the name of the kid, but he couldn't catch her eyes. She was too busy looking around the room, like someone seeking an escape route. "It was his mother's idea, not mine. I wanted something simple, like Gaydrian."

Jonas's son made a retching face at hearing the name his father wanted him to have and folded his arms flat in front of his chest.

"Oh well," Jonas noted. "What about yours?"

"I'm Jason, and this quiet lady is Sabrina." Sabrina lifted her hand in a waving fashion before letting it fall flat on her side. She then took a seat on the armrest of the couch, messing with the calculator watch on her wrist. Jonas waited a few moments while periodically looking at the bear. Finally, Jason got a clue. "Oh and this little guy is, uh, Teddy." The bear gave a toothy grin as it happily played in Jason's hair.

"Teddy, the bear—how creative. So why don't we get down to business and talk about punishments? Sabrina." Jonas looked over at her. She had finally stopped messing with the watch, as if accepting defeat. "For altering dimensions and stealing from a dimension, I hereby sentence you to a date with my son, Trandon."

Sabrina's eyes opened wide, and she froze in place. Trandon, on the other hand, stood rather abruptly with a big smile on his face. Both Teddy and Jason hid their grins unwell.

"Stay seated, my boy; I'm only kidding. And you relax, girl."

Trandon grumbled as he returned to his seat while Sabrina breathed a sigh of relief. "No, you will have to return what you have stolen and right a number of other wrongs."

"Fine, here is what I took, take it!" Sabrina pulled out the Statue of Liberty pen she had been holding onto in her pocket and tried to give it to the man.

"What? No. Why'd you take a souvenir pen?" Jonas inspected it momentarily before handing it back. "I'm talking about Jason here."

"What?" Simultaneously Jason and Sabrina questioned his statement.

"Yes, Jason. Return him to his dimension and do some other tasks, and you'll be off the hook. Simple?"

"Yeah," Sabrina responded.

"Good! Then afterward, you can return to your dimension to stay for good this time."

Sabrina lowered her head.

Jason thought for a moment, realizing he had never asked to go anywhere with Sabrina. She practically had stolen him, but he wasn't complaining.

"Wait. What dimension are you from?" Jason piped in, snapping back into reality.

"The Evil-Plotters Dimension, of course. She didn't tell you? Usually, they reveal that once they are going through with a master plan that could be foiled at any minute," Jonas responded.

"Okay, what do I have to do?" Sabrina interrupted, her face looking a bit red, as if embarrassed.

"Well, you first will have to return this poor man to his own dimension and let him mend the things in his life that were changed by all your dimensional jumps," Jonas stated. "I've seen some of the footage of what happened. It isn't pretty."

Sabrina looked at Jason, and her eyes dropped down toward the floor after he caught her gaze. Jason hadn't ever seen her like this. He was concerned. For the duration of time he'd known her, she had lived as if she knew being caught would bring punishment, but now that she was being punished, she was acting like a child. He didn't know why he decided to say what he did next, but he felt it was the right thing for him to do.

"Let me help her. It'll make this go by more smoothly to have someone helping her," Jason suggested, making Sabrina perk up a bit. Trandon looked surprised and then a little angry, perhaps wishing he made the suggestion first. Jonas looked at Jason, letting a few moments tick by.

"All right then, it is your time that will be wasted. Of course, due to the mechanics of how you will be traveling, you will be upsetting other people's dimensions momentarily. So we'll go through these issues one at a time and when things are convenient." Jonas stated as he used the remote to change the images on the screen.

"What are the mechanics?" Jason questioned.

Trandon scoffed. "You've been carrying around a Personal Dimensional Transporter, and you don't know anything about it? Gah, no wonder so many dimensions are screwed up," Trandon said with another scoff.

Jonas butted in, hushing his son with his hand. "When you used that Personal Dimensional Transporter, you assumed the physical body of yourself in the dimension you traveled to. Whoever was in the dimension you went to, swapped to wherever you came from. If you hadn't existed in a dimension, then you would have assumed your own self in every way. In most cases, dimensional selves mimic movement, so that is why you found yourself in very similar places when traveling."

"So, that would explain all the crazy things going on at my parents' house, right?" Jason inquired as he tried to grasp at what Jonas was talking about.

"Indeed, at least most of them," Jonas responded, changing images on the screen with the remote. A few more moments passed in silent thought as Jonas shifted through the pictures on the television until it showed a group of individuals setting up what looked like a convention room with a podium and hundreds of chairs.

"Here is the first and perhaps most straightforward task. The man scheduled to speak at this event they are preparing for isn't acting himself. Due to a dimensional incident, the correct personality is trapped in another dimension. You must go there and retrieve him, returning him to his proper dimension. Simple?"

Sabrina nodded as Jason stood up, ready to go.

"Great, let us do this!" Fired up and trying to get Sabrina pumped, Jason started walking to the stairs they had come up.

"All right, that is the spirit, but I will need about an hour to get things prepared," Jonas responded as he then began fiddling with the remote. "Entertain yourselves for a bit!"

Jason looked a bit let down that his burst of energy was wasted. He then sat back down on the couch where he tried to watch the television as Jonas worked, but it was no longer on any pictures but rather lots of text that was hard for Jason to follow. So he instead spent the next while with his eyes closed, snoozing.

"Got it! Let me you get you the dimensional codes!" Jonas yelled, waking Jason from his nap. He then stood and headed back into his room.

"C … codes?" Jason questioned, slowly waking up. Sabrina was off in a corner, and Trandon looked wide awake, having just scoffed again after what Jason said and opened his mouth to speak.

"Codes … the things you enter into the watch," Jonas responded quickly as if preempting Trandon. He came back out of his room with a piece of scrap paper in hand, writing on it. He then handed it over to Jason. "You see, the watch you possess can have up to ten digits entered into it. The first seven determine a dimension, while the last three are the time slots in minutes of how long to stay in the dimension. Got it?"

Jason shook his head in confusion.

"Then let Sabrina handle it." Jonas directed.

Jason eyed the paper, reading in his head, *4583920030*. He then looked at Jonas and asked, "Thirty minutes? Are you sure that is long enough to find someone?"

"Yes," Jonas replied. "It is very easy to find the odd man out in a dimension, especially the one you are going to. Not to mention, I have his area sort of pinpointed out and have managed to get your alter-dimensional selves close by."

"So who are we getting, and where are we taking them?" Jason asked valid questions.

"Ah yes, here you go." On another piece of scrap paper, Jonas wrote some more information. He then handed the piece of paper to Sabrina. "You can take it, as you are the one being punished." Sabrina pocketed the information, not even looking at it.

Sabrina then snatched the paper with the dimensional codes on it from Jason's hand, quickly running her eyes over the numbers. "So, how do we get out of here? I've tried the watch a dozen times with no luck."

Jonas had already started walking to the door to his room. He then turned his head toward Jason and Sabrina. "That is because no one can get out of here unless they are let out. Try the numbers I gave you, and you'll be able to go." Jonas made a few steps into his room before calling out to Sabrina, "And I don't recommend using your pin to go anywhere else when you travel to these dimensions. I won't be as kind next time." He laughed a hearty laugh before returning to his chair.

Trandon went back to flipping through images on the television.

"How will you know if I use it?" Sabrina asked.

"I got you here, didn't I?" Jonas retorted. "Don't worry, dimensional travel is carefully watched. Well, sort of at least." Jonas eyed in the direction of his son before returning his bowler hat to the on-his-face position and reclining in his chair.

Jason took Teddy off of his shoulders momentarily, due to the bear's fur causing his neck to sweat, and placed him on the couch next to Trandon. The bear sat there watching the television.

"Never thought the law would catch up with you, huh?" Jason asked Sabrina with a smile.

"I never thought the law *could* catch up with me," Sabrina responded. "I guess I was wrong, as I have been about so many things in my life." She showed a vulnerable side that Jason had never seen in either this version of Sabrina or the other.

"We will fix these things. Surely the list isn't that long."

"Well …" Sabrina fidgeted with the paper in her hands.

"Well what?" Jason asked, hoping he wasn't going to regret helping her out.

"Let us just say I've had the watch for some time now, and even though I haven't been intentionally messing up lives in every dimension I visited, there are still some issues caused by dimension traveling this way."

"Such as the broken picture frames in my parents' house and my mom putting her powder on my bed?"

"What?"

"Never mind. Why don't we just start with this one and go from there?"

Sabrina shrugged at Jason. "Why not?" She then lifted her leg up a few inches off the ground. Jason looked down at it, feeling sort of demeaned. "Come on, I'm raising it as high as I can. Just grab it so we can get this over with."

Jason reached down and grabbed on to her ankle. Sabrina took an inordinate amount of time inputting numbers into the watch, almost as if she didn't even want to do what the man said and would sooner take her chances with Trandon.

Jason wasn't quite sure the dimensional jump had happened until he opened his eyes, having shut them out of habit, and saw that they were inside of a coffee shop. *Ha-ha,* he thought, *no more pain.* He still felt a little light headed, though. Oops, he just fell out of the chair he was sitting in.

CHAPTER 7

---※---

After receiving assistance from Sabrina back into his seat, a familiar scene with Jason by now, Jason took a look at the layout around him. The coffee shop they sat in was quite plain with simple round-topped tables, comfy black chairs, and a lady behind the bar dressed as a mime.

Jason turned his head to look at Sabrina and noticed that she was dressed as a mime too, with a black tear painted below her left eye. How fitting. Jason opened his mouth to talk but found himself unwilling to. *Great. What now?* he asked his curious little mind.

He waved his hand in front of Sabrina, trying to get her attention. She was too busy covering her mouth as if she were attempting to hold in a laugh. What had her in such a laughing frenzy? It could have possibly been the girl behind the bar and the way she was dressed. Who knows with Sabrina. When she turned and saw Jason, she mimicked slapping her hand on the table, then on her leg, and then actually started rolling on the floor. All of this was done while pretending to laugh loudly.

How odd, Jason thought. He realized rather quickly where they must be—the Mime Dimension. *Dang it. This is going to take some time.*

Jason did a rope-pulling mimic to help Sabrina off of the floor. She followed suit, pulling herself up. Once she was standing, Sabrina held her sides as if she had laughed too hard. Funny. Her goofing off was beginning to wear on Jason. He wanted to locate the person they needed to get, mime their way into an understanding of the predicament, and then return the person back to his own dimension.

Jason had a fleeting feeling that by doing this deed, he'd become some sort of hero, like a super mime—righting what was wrong and fixing the problems caused by the wicked. Even if that were the case, he was hanging with the evil person. *Wait. What is Sabrina doing now?* She had started doing the box trick where she placed her hands in front of herself flat and then above and to the sides, mimicking that she was stuck in an invisible box. *That is impressive*, he thought. *Almost as good as her robot moves.*

Jason suddenly realized that he didn't feel any weight on his shoulders. *Where did Teddy go?* He briefly forgot that he left Teddy on the couch next to Trandon, the poor little guy. This made Jason feel like a neglectful super mime.

Jason mimed to Sabrina to open up her pocket and look for the scrap paper. She was too busy turning her invisible box into an octagon. How would she ever get out? Oh, she created a door. Good.

After a few moments, Sabrina reached into her pocket and pulled out a piece of paper and examined it, making a relatively funny face while doing so. Jason peaked over her shoulder and saw words that read HAROLD DEE PACKER. How were they ever going to find this person without verbally asking anyone?

Sabrina quickly walked over to the mime behind the counter, who she was probably laughing at earlier, and showed her the scrap paper. The lady behind the counter must have seen Sabrina's fit of laughter, because instead of being civil, she mimicked closing a door in Sabrina's face.

It is possible that the lady's abrupt rudeness was due to her having to work. You see, in this dimension, there are few actual jobs, seeing as most people just mime around. They rotate who is working—who gets to be mime president, who serves coffee for the day, who is the mime mom and dad. I'm sure some of these mimes would get upset being stuck at one place all day, unable to lasso people. That is, unless they were pretending to be a cowboy. Then they could lasso all day.

One person down, an infinite number left to go, Jason thought. He did notice that there was a name tag on the outfit of the lady mime behind the counter before he headed for the exit. Sabrina tried knocking on the invisible door the woman had slammed in her face but ended up just making a rude gesture through an imaginary window she created.

Outside on the streets, the town itself didn't look much different than any typical city, aside from the denizens, of course. Every person shared the same white painted face and striped clothing. They differed in a choice of color for the lips and eyes; some wore top hats, and others didn't. The stripes on their clothing differed in color, as well as their pants and shoes.

Jason was amazed by the variety of mime outfits, while Sabrina seemed to enjoy creating objects with the movement of her hands. Jason turned to see her finishing her latest creation, the bicycle built for two. Sabrina mimicked getting onto the bike. She then motioned Jason to get on behind her. He shook his hand in dismissal and instead started walking along the sidewalk toward two crossing streets. He took a gander to either side, recalling that Jonas stuck them here because their target was close.

At the intersection of the two streets, there was much activity. Jason started to check name tags as mimes walked by but came to realize he had forgotten the name of the person already. Just a few seconds of looking later, with a grin on her face, came Sabrina mimicking riding the bicycle. When she got close to Jason, she pretended to chime a bell on the invisible handlebars in her hands. With a quick reversal of her arm, Sabrina once again made a patting motion to show Jason there was room on this ride for another.

He finally caved in, deciding to indulge the funny bone and partake in an evening ride. Jason mimicked getting onto the backseat, placing his hands on the imaginary handlebars in front of him and mimicked peddling forward. He figured Sabrina would join in too; after all, she was watching him. Sabrina just shook her head when Jason ran into the back of her and mimed for him to put on his helmet. *Of all the ridiculous things*, Jason thought as he, not for the last time, regretted being nice by offering to help Sabrina out.

Sabrina pretended to put on goggles. She then mimicked making sure Jason's helmet was on tight, because imaginary biking reaches insane speeds, and then they were off. By lifting their knees almost in march, they simulated riding a bicycle down the many sidewalks. On the other side of the street, two mimes actually rode bicycles. Figures.

As they kept moving down the path, Sabrina would pull out the paper and show it to other mimes. Some would respond by boxing themselves in, and others would act as if they were pulling earbuds out of their ears, each done before shrugging and shaking their heads. Jason at first wondered why she skipped so many people but was glad, because after just a few mimes, he was already annoyed.

They hadn't done much seeking before Sabrina picked a fight. She tossed the imaginary bike down and squared off in a boxing match against another mime. Jason was too busy pumping up her shoulders to notice the sizeable crowd that had gathered. The mime Sabrina was engaging had made some rude gestures to the two of them and ripped the scrap paper in half when they had shown it to her.

At first, the other mime made punches at the air as if simulating warming up before a match, but then it got far too real. Sabrina came in with a left hook and caught the jaw of the skinny, flat-chested female mime. This sent the poor girl to the ground. There she coughed up a small portion of blood. Jason walked between Sabrina and the fallen girl, pretending to hold up a round sign.

After making his walk across, Jason got down on his knees and mimicked slapping the ground as if counting to see if the other mime would get up; she was unable to. Jason stood and grabbed Sabrina's arm, raising it high in the air. It was a flawless victory for Sabrina.

Then there was the shocked looks from the crowd and a mime doctor or two, and a group of self-proclaimed police mimes showed up on the scene. All mime fingers pointed at Sabrina, including Jason's. One of the police mimes proceeded to lasso Sabrina and pull her in, but Jason thought quickly. He pulled out his imaginary knife and mimicked cutting the imaginary rope. For comedic purposes, he pretended to saw the rope with the knife, bite at it, and finally kick it until it broke.

After being released from the invisible rope, Sabrina swooped down, picked up the two strips of paper that formed their information sheet, and pocketed them. She and Jason then fled quite rapidly and managed to lose the two police mimes who had given chase. The police mimes pretended to get tired and need a donut break.

After a few moments of side holding and mimicking high amounts of laughter, Jason and Sabrina once again returned to their trek down the sidewalks of these seemingly endless streets.

While they walked, they kept joking back and forth. Jason's mood had improved significantly. Oh look, Sabrina caught a sidewalk fish. They both seemed to have forgotten why they were there because they no longer checked name badges or started any fights.

After what could have been an hour, but I'm guessing was more like ten minutes, they came to a large gathering of people. A woman pretending to blow a whistle while holding out her other hand in front of her was trying to disperse the crowd without any luck.

It was odd to see her and the few others doing this because none of them could be determined differently from any other mime. In fact, it was known by others, although not by Jason and Sabrina, that mimes in this dimension could just take on whatever role in society they felt like for that moment. It became confusing when you'd have someone start as an arsonist and cause a fire, only to pretend to be a firefighter a few seconds later and end up being the large man in the tub who needs rescuing.

This whole situation was different from the actual job portion of the dimension because people couldn't just stop doing their real job when they wanted, thus why they were grumpy in doing the job. No one ever said that other dimensions would make sense, so there is no use complaining.

"What ... what are you doing? This doesn't make any sense." What did I just say about making sense? "I feel like I am stuck in some sort of cartoon without any audio!" A man's voice could be heard from the center of the crowd. Multiple mimes mimicked plugging up their ears, and even a few did so for their kids. Sabrina pushed forward through the crowd with Jason in tow.

When they made it to the center of the group, they saw the man who had been yelling being pulled into a vehicle. His eyes showed a look of bewilderment as if he thought he was the only sane person in the world. The people pulling him were dressed as mimes wearing sunshades, ties, and ear pieces. Was this the mime Secret Service? Why would they need ear pieces if they weren't supposed to make sounds? Not to worry, Jason asks questions like this all of the time. Most the time he gets an answer—most of the time.

Sabrina pulled out the two strips of paper that formed their information sheet. She then placed them together so that they formed the full name of the person they were looking for. She then ran up to the man as he was being dragged backward toward the car. A quick glance at his name tag, and surely she knew that they matched. She motioned Jason to assist her.

Jason and Sabrina tried a number of tricks to stop the Secret Service mimes from dragging off poor, confused Harold. They started by pretending to lasso Harold and were even able to get the mimes in black to pretend to have a tug of war with them, at least until Jason slipped on an imaginary banana.

Sabrina then attempted to knock out one of the Secret Service mimes. At first, she pretended to, and then she really was about to hit one over the head but was stopped by Jason.

They were both worn out from all their failed attempts and very near the vehicle when Jason had an idea. "Hey, Sabrina, I have an idea!" he announced and was soon the center of attention of the mime crowd. The Secret Service mimes took notice too and grabbed Jason. They didn't mess around with their grappling either. No use of imaginary holding devices, just raw strength that Jason couldn't struggle out of.

"Brilliant!" Sabrina yelled after seeing Jason being pulled toward the vehicle too. She quickly covered her mouth and tried to act like someone else had talked, but the Secret Service mimes grabbed her too. They were both tossed into the back of the vehicle with Harold, sitting side by side; the door shut and locked from the outside. Sabrina looked at Jason and said in a genuinely sincere voice, "Good idea!"

It was rather dark inside the vehicle due to the tinted windows and black cloth seats. Two mimes sat in the front seats of the car. They both wore shades and ear pieces. One of the mimes mimicked that there was an invisible wall between the sections of the vehicle and that the three of them should keep their mouths shut.

"You two talk as well!" Harold exasperated. He had broken out into a light sweat from all the struggling and proceeded to wipe it away with a black beret that had been on top of his very short salt-and-pepper hair. Harold wore clothes that were just as ridiculous as the rest—black pants, striped shirt, red scarf, and white gloves. His ebony skin wrinkled as he smiled, showing pearly white teeth to everyone in the vehicle

Both of the Secret Service mimes glanced back at them, frowning significantly. Jason nodded at Harold as Sabrina looked over the sheet of paper with the dimensional codes on it. She studied the piece of paper for a few moments. I admit the handwriting wasn't the best, but she didn't need to pretend to put on glasses.

"Yes, we speak." Sabrina finally responded to the overjoyed Harold.

"That is fantastic! I can't get a word out of these other blokes. All they do is create boxes and lasso each other back and forth. It was strange at first because I felt obliged to follow along, but soon I broke this darned curse. And it seems you have too! Now, what was your idea, son?" Harold's brown eyes opened wide as he looked at Jason.

"Honestly, I hadn't thought too hard about it."

"Well, surely we could appeal to the system of law here?"

"I'm not sure if that'd work," Jason replied, pondering for a moment how a mime courtroom would work. Without any sound, how would the judge get order restored? Then again, how would disorder start? It would probably begin with a fist fight and involve Sabrina.

"So you are Harold Dee Packer, correct?" Sabrina butted into their conversation, apparently getting down to business. Harold turned to face Sabrina and nodded.

"How do you know my real name?" Harold asked.

Jason looked at Harold, noticing that his name tag read TIMMY, THE SAD SANTA. Jason then looked at Sabrina.

"And how did you know this was our guy?"

"I didn't," Sabrina responded rather shortly. "I just figured he'd stand out like the sorest of thumbs." She glanced at the numbers on the scrap paper and typed them into the calculator watch before pocketing the paper and laying her legs across both Harold and Jason. Jason latched his arms around one of her ankles. He then motioned for Harold to follow suit.

"I get what you are talking about, KAREN, QUEEN OF CRYING," Harold replied, reading Sabrina's nametag. Sabrina looked down at her nametag and then ripped it off. "It took a lot of strength to start talking. For the longest time, I was making screeching sounds!" He then looked down at Sabrina's leg. "Why are we grabbing onto Karen's ankles?" Harold asked Jason.

The Secret Service mimes kept glancing back at the trio. They looked annoyed. One even pretended to open a door on the invisible wall that separated the two halves of the car and wagged his finger at them. Jason looked over at Harold, again motioning him to grab hold of Sabrina's ankle. Harold dropped his head and sighed, grabbing onto Sabrina's other ankle.

Within seconds, it was over, and they no longer wore those awful outfits. Harold didn't take the dimensional jump well and almost vomited, while Jason held up decent enough, and Sabrina seemed to have no reaction as usual. They were still riding in the backseat of a vehicle, only now their clothes were different. They had been changed into business attire.

"Sir, are you feeling all right?" A voice came from the front of the vehicle.

"Oh yes, done it a few times now, and things hurt less." Jason responded to the question that was apparently not directed at him. The man rephrased his question, ensuring to include Mr. Packer at the end.

"Yes, yes never better! We are allowed to talk now, aren't we? Good! Where are we headed?" Harold asked. His face was one gigantic smile, having just looked at his attire. The driver responded rather unsure, as if a joke were being played on him, and told Harold they were heading to a conference in which Harold was to speak for his company. "Ah yes! That conference. Aren't we a little late, though?" Harold asked, checking his watch.

Sabrina retracted her ankles, so only one sat on Jason's lap now.

"Well, sir, we would have been there by now, but you wouldn't talk for the longest of times. You kept making hand motions. We didn't know what to make of it, sir," the driver responded, apparently relieved that whatever nightmare had been going on was finally over. "Oh, and you indicated for me to bring along these two. Are they friends of yours?"

"I dare say they are better than friends!" Harold responded, obviously cheerful.

Jason smiled, knowing it was a job well done.

Harold thanked Jason and Sabrina for returning him home and asked that they never fill him in on the details of how it happened. He iterated multiple times that whatever crazy thing happened, be it in his mind or real events, it'd be best to stay a nightmare and nothing more.

Sabrina waved her leg in front of Jason's face. *What, already?* Jason thought.

"If you want to be left behind, feel free just to look at it," Sabrina smirked as she watched the countdown on the watch. It had been set only to allow them a few minutes of time here.

Jason grabbed hold of her leg, and Harold started to do so too rather mindlessly. He had begun a lengthy rant on the kookiness of a mime community and how it might work for a theme park, at least until you wanted to punch one. Sabrina noticed him trying to latch on to her leg and pulled it back rather quickly, forcing Jason to fall into her lap. She just grinned down at Jason and said, "Why hello there."

The dimensional jump ended as soon as it had begun, with both Jason and Sabrina finding that they were sitting on the floor beside the lamppost. Well, Sabrina was sitting, and Jason was lying on her lap. Jason got up rather abruptly, as if he would feel embarrassed to get caught in that position with her. Sabrina just half-grinned. Jason then dusted some imaginary dirt off of himself, forgetting he wasn't in the Mime Dimension anymore.

"It looks like the old kook was right, after all," Sabrina stated after having stood up. Jason looked questioningly at her. "It brought us back here. I was skeptical and thought we'd be spending an evening miming out our feelings for each other." Jason felt even more embarrassed after that, but he smiled anyway. "I'm just kidding, you idiot." Sabrina gave Jason a hearty punch to his arm and started walking toward the stairs, Jason lagging behind slightly.

"You don't mind doing this kind of stuff? Or mind that I tagged along?" Jason spoke out, lingering near the lamppost. Sabrina turned around from her position at the bottom of the stairs, looking as if she were thinking for a moment.

"This guy up here seems to have control over dimensional travel. I'm not sure how, but I know that if I want to have some freedom, I'll have to pay for my crimes." She added quotes to the last word there, apparently not believing what she did was all that bad. Besides, the only things she took were the souvenir pen and a person. She turned to walk up the stairs. "Oh, and I like having you along. Otherwise, I'm sure Trandon would've weaseled his way into helping."

Jason knew that was one of the nicer comments out of her, so he took it and followed her up the stairs.

CHAPTER 8

"I haven't had quite enough time to sort out all the details for the next pressing matter. I admit that I have been sleeping. So you will all have to sit and quietly discuss important events. Here is a subject for your discussion." Jonas stopped pacing and pointed to a magazine with a picture of Trandon's favorite female celebrity on the cover. "Of course, I had expected you two to spend more time goofing off in the Mime Dimension. You could've knocked out at least two more people, Sabrina." Jonas gave her a wink.

"I would have had to if I hadn't found Harold as fast as I did," Sabrina stated, ignoring that Jason was there to help. "And you could've given us his mime name."

"I could have ..." Jonas responded as he walked off.

After his father had left the room, Trandon began discussing all sorts of reasons to like the celebrity his dad suggested as a subject. He even compared her beauty to Sabrina's. Teddy munched on some cheese-covered crisp snacks that he got from a bag Trandon had been eating from. You know, I'm not sure if the bear is male or female, but whatever it is, it's making a sizable mess all over Jason's lap and the floor.

I've got a cute animal in my lap, a pervert to my left, and a devious alter-dimensional version of one of my good friends to my right. I am pretty sure I left the lights on in my vehicle ... Wait. When did I last drive it? Cara isn't driving it right now, is she? What if an alter-dimensional version of me has driven it? Jason's mind raced, not wanting to hear about Trandon's fantasies.

Sabrina pulled out the Statue of Liberty pen. She twirled it between her fingers for a moment before tossing it into a nearby wastebasket. She then rested her arm on her knee and head in hand. She looked to be bothered by something.

It took some time for Jason to notice this obvious sign of displeasure and to register the tossing of the pen. I believe it was the fourth or fifth audible sigh from Sabrina that broke Jason's thought trance. He looked over at her. His eyes adjusted from their glazed, staring-off-into-emptiness state to one that showed he was all there in his mind.

"So, why'd you take that souvenir pen anyway, and were you chased?" Jason asked with a lighthearted laugh. Sabrina smiled, but Jason saw past her fake smile. "No, really. Please tell me." Her attitude may have been different, but her facial features were the same as the Sabrina he knew from his dimension. Again, his mind wandered, wondering where the other Sabrina might be right now. Jason was pulled from his new train of thought by an elbow nudge from Sabrina, a bit of a forceful jab actually.

"In the dimension I came from, we all have evil plots that we want to carry out. This gets old when everyone you know is trying the same things to each other. So my master thought it'd be clever if we found a hidden way to another dimension, hidden because our dimension's ingoing and outgoing traffic is monitored heavily. Upon finding a way out, he thought we could then steal something that exists in the dimension we reach that doesn't exist in ours, seeing as everything of significant value in my home dimension has been destroyed or stolen. To make the story short, we were able to get our hands on the watch, and I was tasked with taking some valuable object from a random dimension I went to." Sabrina stopped talking, looking down at her hands as she fidgeted with her fingernails.

"So you took the Statue of Liberty pen," Jason stated, trying to get Sabrina to keep talking. More time passed before Sabrina looked up and sighed.

"I knew it wasn't the real deal. I am such a lousy apprentice. My stepsister is so much better at this than me. I just wanted to take back something—anything, really. I mean we worked so hard to get the PDT." Sabrina again lowered her head, and for the first time since he met this dimensional personality of Sabrina, Jason felt sorry for her.

"Your stepsister?"

"Yeah, she is the typical one you'd expect a screwup like me to have. She is beautiful, smart, and can sing. Not to mention she does things right."

"I would say I know what you are talking about, but you met my sister," Jason said, mimicking Sabrina's posture with his head now resting on his hand. "Well, you met a version of my sister that talks and acts like a robot."

"Yeah … I can only imagine what the one from your dimension is like. I would have done worse than just push her down."

"Is there a version of you that isn't violent?"

"Nope," Sabrina said with a grin.

"Well, at least we know your dimensional selves have a similar quality." Jason has a great way with words, again demonstrated here. Sabrina just laughed at what Jason said and looked at him with a lingering stare but soon broke the awkwardness by glancing at Trandon, who was staring at them both. He looked appalled.

"Whoa, I was talking! Where are your manners? I can't believe you would stop listening to me talk about this remarkable woman!" Trandon ranted.

Jonas reentered the room at a quick pace. He was staring down at some pieces of paper in his hands and was not paying attention to where he was going. After making a few quick steps, he bumped his pelvis region into the back of the couch. This sent Teddy to the floor in shock. Jonas grumbled his excuses to Teddy and wedged himself on the sofa in between Jason and Sabrina.

"Okay, I have a series of wrongs to be righted. Which one do you want to do first?" Jonas said as he held up the papers like a magician would do with cards.

"Hold on, hold on. Quick question," Jason interrupted. "When we went to the Mime Dimension, did those mimes come here?" I told you Jason's mind had been wandering.

"No, they went to Harold's dimension because that is where I had them sent when you went to the Mime Dimension. In the case of this dimension, no one comes here but those who are allowed. It is like an exclusive club without the awesome parties, liquor, cool adventures, and everything that makes a club fun," Jonas responded, having donned glasses. He was looking over them at Jason.

"Okay then. When we left the Mime Dimension, what happened to the mimes that regained their bodies?"

"You mean the ones in the car?" Jason nodded. "They will be okay. Once they show they are indeed silent. Got any other questions on that boiling mind of yours? Nope? Good." Jonas took the glasses off and set them aside before taking control of the remote and changing the image on the television.

He started to talk about the next assignments. There were more poor souls who need saving from dimensional mix-ups. All the while, he kept mentioning how dimensional travel needs to be better monitored. Jason inquired, still with his mind steadily burning, how exactly it is watched in the first place. He understood that Trandon would come here when school got out and watch the television for his dad, but how do they watch it all? Plus how do people find out about it?

Jonas explained that in a Control Dimension, similar to the one that Jason is from, people aren't allowed to know about dimensional travel. It is like an experiment that he is a part of. Also, there is some sort of dimensional law, written in a dimensional code book, held somewhere secret that prevents the spreading of said experimental knowledge. He further talked about how people from other dimensions are given the option to travel to a Control Dimension.

"Wait a minute ... you said *a* Control Dimension. There are more than one?" Jason inquired.

"There are more than one—fifteen to be more precise. You have been to two of them; Control Dimension 05 and Control Dimension 02. The second being the Opposite Dimension you slipped into."

"Opposite Dimension?"

"An Opposite Dimension is a dimension that is the replica of another Control Dimension, except everything has been inverted. Well, not everything, just each person in either dimension has entirely different personalities from each other."

"Okay, so my dimension is number five then," Jason said, trying to make sense of all of this. That was all he was capable of understanding at the moment.

"You could say that. Each Control Dimension has people from other dimensions, and we have so many that if one dimension is no longer worth keeping, we can just ..." Jonas seemed to trail off into thought.

Jason looked at him, expecting him to finish.

When the silence had gone on for too long, Jonas started rambling about what they needed to do to finish up Sabrina's punishment. "Now there are quite a few issues to be sorted out, but to keep us from becoming overwhelmed, I've picked the most urgent."

Jason watched as Jonas, using the remote control, changed the television screen to depict a man saving a woman from a fire. The man wore a green body suit with a golden *L* imprinted on his chest. Holes were cut out in the head portion of the suit for his eyes, nostrils, and mouth. He also wore golden boots, gloves, and what looked to be golden boxers over the latex suit.

"His name is Leo," Jonas stated.

"Leo? Not Laserman or something cool?" Jason asked, realizing quickly this person was pretending to be a superhero with a very ordinary name.

"Just Leo. He comes from a dimension where everyone has what your Control Dimension would call super powers and also strong desires for justice."

"And apparently bad taste when it comes to clothes," Sabrina said, folding her arms in front of her chest.

"Now don't be hateful because your dimension no longer has free access to this dimension."

"Free access? You guys weren't their villains, were you?" Jason looked past Jonas at Sabrina, seriously thinking this was all being made up.

"One could say that to have justice, you have to have injustice. Sabrina's dimension provided that for a while. It got out of hand, so both sides had to be put into time-outs. It seems they are getting bored in, we'll call it, the Superhero Dimension and are finding ways to other dimensions so they might do justice there." Jonas flipped between views of the burning building as the man in green moved very quickly throughout it, grabbing people and dropping them off outside.

"I don't think that is a bad thing, you know? Sometimes people need saving." Jason attempted to reason, having a strong sense of justice within himself.

"In many typical cases, I'd agree with you, but this situation isn't usual, as most cases around here tend not to be. The dimension he is in is a dimension that is most odd and usually kept from people going in and out of."

"Why?"

"'Cause it is the Immortal Dimension." Trandon butted in.

"That is your nickname for it. It is properly called dimension … never mind. We'll call it the Immortal Dimension. Essentially in this dimension no one can die from anything, except old age. Leo will drive himself insane if he continues trying to save people because they don't worry if a building is burning to the ground or if they are drowning." Jonas stopped using the remote. The screen showed a view of Leo, who was worn out from carrying people out of the building. Funny enough, many of the people whom he brought out ran right back in. "You see? So you'll go there, get him, and take him back to his own dimension."

"Okay, I'm confused again. Why is Leo still wearing his superhero uniform when he is in another dimension? Wouldn't he assume his dimensional self in the Immortal Dimension?" Jason asked.

Sabrina stood up, messing with the calculator watch. She began to wander about, restlessly.

"In most cases, dimensions will have an alternate version of you in them. In most instances. Even in an Immortal Dimension, things can happen that prevent alternative versions from continuing to exist or even having come to exist," Jonas replied as he lowered his head. He then rather quickly lifted it back up. "No need to bring the party down. Let me get a new sheet of paper and write everything you need to know about this adventure on it. This one is covered in doodles." Indeed, the paper in his hand did have a few stick figures drawn on it.

Jonas stood up and returned to his room. Jason looked at Sabrina and saw that she had left to go back down the stairs. He too stood up, leaving Trandon and Teddy with the television and remote, and began following after Sabrina. Down the stairs, he could see Sabrina leaning against the fence that surrounded the lamppost. She kept fiddling with the watch and periodically glanced at the twinkling stars. Jason walked up to her side, placing a hand on her shoulder.

"What is up?"

"What do you mean, *what is up?*" Sabrina responded, emphasizing the words Jason said to her.

"I mean, why did you walk away?"

"I don't get emotional Jason, if that is what you are after. I came here to think before Jonas came back."

"Think about what?" Jason thought he hit a nerve because Sabrina scowled and turned away from him. "It has been a long day. Do you want to see about continuing to pay off your debt another day?"

"No."

"Then what do you want?"

"I … I want what you have, Jason. I want your control, your naivety."

"My what?" Jason rested his arms on the fence too, looking out at the stars.

"You don't understand how hard it is to constantly feel like you have to prove yourself. To feel like if you screw up, you won't be able to return home without shame." Sabrina explained as she removed the calculator watch from her wrist, dangling it over the fence.

"I don't?" Jason squinted one of his eyes, placed his hand out arm's length, and then acted as if he were squishing a star with his fingers. "You saw my home life and have met my parents. I'm anything but accomplished. I could add dimensional travel to my resume, but I doubt it'd help me!"

Sabrina laughed and then looked at Jason as he looked at her. "You know what would make me happy?" she asked, looking deep into Jason's eyes.

"What?" he responded and then took a deep gulp of air as his heart began to nervously race, her face getting closer to his.

"This." Sabrina dropped the calculator watch from her hand, letting it fall past what possibly could be the bottom of whatever they were standing on. Jason looked dumbfounded, expecting something to be going on in the general direction of Sabrina's face, but he soon realized what she had done. He took a few steps back and began frantically reaching through the bars of the fence as if he could grab the watch before it slipped too far away.

"Sabrina! Why'd you do that? Jonas isn't going to be happy with you. He may never let you leave your dimension!" Jason said as he stood, unable to believe what Sabrina had just done.

"I know." She then forcefully reached out her right hand, grabbing Jason's shirt and pulling him closer to her for a kiss. They locked lips, solidly for a few moments. Eventually, the kiss ended, but Sabrina kept a solid hold on Jason's shirt. She was quite strong and able to keep Jason upright, considering his legs were wobbly now. "I'm not much for good-bye kisses, so consider it me saying thank you for … ow!"

Sabrina was cut short by a metal object smacking her on the head. It then landed on the floor at their feet. Both Jason and Sabrina simultaneously looked down to see what it was that clanked on the floor. Sabrina looked very surprised, and Jason was relieved to see the calculator watch.

"I honestly don't want to know what I'm interrupting," Jonas said from the stairs. He had just come down, paper in hand, and noticed Jason and Sabrina.

"It was just …" Jason started to explain.

"I'm all right, Jason. Trust me. I don't have to know. I can watch it on the television later." Jonas paused for a moment. "That came out creepier than I wanted it to."

Sabrina rubbed the back of her head, having released Jason from her iron grip. She looked up and then down at the ground. Then she looked at Jonas and pointed at him with an accusing finger. "You threw that at me, didn't you?"

"I threw what at you?" Jonas answered back with a question of his own, looking at the sheet of paper.

"The calculator watch, the same one that I dropped over the edge! Is that some kind of punishment? These adventures to fix wrongs are torturous enough. I don't need physical punishment too." Sabrina retorted. "You won't let me opt out either, will you? I can't just get rid of the PDT and be done with it?"

"Why'd you drop the watch?" Jonas asked Sabrina, his demeanor very calm. He then quickly lifted a hand up as if to stop any explanation. "Never mind. I don't want to know. I can watch it later. We are wasting precious time. Here is your information." Jonas moved closer to the two and tried to give Sabrina the sheet of paper, but she didn't take it.

Sabrina stood there fuming, crossing her arms in front of her chest. In my opinion, she was making a bigger deal out of the situation than necessary.

"Since I can see your face is begging to ask a question, Jason, and I can see you aren't going to smile until this is settled, Sabrina, I will try to explain why you were hit in the head by the same PDT that you dropped from that edge." Jonas spoke calmly, looking between the two. He cleared his throat and began to pace. "It was fate, Sabrina—your fate to be precise. Destiny has delivered you a heavy burden, but you must bear it. This is a proving ground. You are destined to carry this burden until your journey is complete. So in answer to your earlier question, no. You cannot just opt out! It may be a troublesome voyage, but you can survive. You have a bit of charisma and plenty of wit. Not to mention, you have this handsome lad to aid you." Jonas stopped in front of Jason, smiling as he wedged the slip of paper with the dimensional information on it between Sabrina's folded arms. He then began to walk off toward the stairs.

"Really?!" Sabrina asked, after having spent a few moments in silence.

"Nope! Dimensional magic and whatnot … enjoy your trip!" Jonas replied as he headed up the stairs.

Jason bent over and picked up the watch. He then wedged it between Sabrina's folded arms.

CHAPTER 9

Jason and Sabrina arrived in the Immortal Dimension in much the same way they had arrived in every other dimension—no applause or anyone caring much. The only difference this time was that they weren't standing next to each other. They weren't even close to each other. Jonas had explained this possibility and how he had to time entry into other dimensions to ensure both Sabrina and Jason's alter-dimensional personalities were close to each other. He also had to use tricks to get the alter-dimensional personalities to travel to where he needed them to be. In this case, he was off. By a mile, I'd guess.

Jason took in his surroundings. He was standing on the sidewalk of a relatively busy street within a bustling city. Large business buildings surrounded where he stood. The people who walked by wore business attire with minor tears in them—tears caused by being immortal and not caring if they were hit by a car or stabbed.

Jason noticed that Sabrina wasn't anywhere in sight, and right in front of him stood the burning building that he'd seen on the television. Both of his hands were in his pockets, and as he pulled them out, he felt something in his right pocket. It was a slip of paper. Jason pulled the paper out and looked it over, noticing it was a lottery ticket. Perhaps this was what Jonas was using to bring both him and Sabrina together. It was, by the way.

A few firemen had shown up to put out the burning building. They weren't using their fire trucks with hoses attached to hydrants, but rather they walked directly into the building while holding blankets. A few parts of the building collapsed on firemen, but they merely helped each other out of the burning rubble as if nothing had happened. Jason watched with an astonished look on his face.

After a few more firemen had succumbed to falling rubble, Jason walked into the building. Did he want to get smashed by falling debris? Maybe so; he has a knack for trying out whatever a dimension's theme is. Let us see what happens. Yeah, he was just crushed under a pile of rubble.

One of the firemen who already had building pieces fall on him assisted Jason up. He then looked at the smiling young man and said, "Leave this to the professionals. You don't want to spend the rest of your life trapped under some rubble!"

Jason nodded at the fireman before watching him walk off to assist another fireman. Jason spent awhile longer in the burning building, not heeding the words of the fireman. Why should he? After all, there was no threat to life or limb. At worst, he'd be trapped under rubble for a few hours, days, or weeks.

After crashing through the ceiling in multiple places, Jason finally decided to leave the building. It was getting hard to see due to the smoke, and just about everyone else had stopped entering, leaving, and getting trapped under debris. When back out in the sun, Jason came to realize a few things; he was soaked through with sweat, his clothes were covered in soot and charred, and he was extremely thirsty. Not to mention it felt much cooler to him outside than it did in the burning building. Imagine that.

Jason stood there, watching firefighters exit the building with their blankets. It isn't proper procedure in many dimensions for firefighters not to use a fire hose to put out fires, and I believe it is encouraged for them to use one. This dimension is already shaping up to be a bit off. Oh look, they are using the hose to fill up cups with water. Jason partook in some of the refreshing cold water. Even though he quenched his great thirst with the water, he didn't feel satisfied with doing so. Perhaps being immortal meant the body responded differently to what normally would be a necessity to survive.

"There you are! Isn't this fun?" Sabrina approached Jason, having just come out of the burning building. In action-movie fashion, the building collapsed to the ground as she walked out of it. It would have been cool if it also exploded, but we can't get everything we want.

"It is so much fun! Want to jump off a cliff?" Jason responded, his adrenaline still pumping.

"Normally, I'm more akin to pushing people off of cliffs while their feet and hands are bound, but I can make an exception," Sabrina replied between gulps of water. It seemed any aggression she had displayed before coming to this dimension had vanished. Kind of like a kid who just got hit by a ball and started to cry, but then someone gave the kid a sucker to shut the kid up.

"A while back if you had said that to me, I would've avoided you, but now … now I just want to get to that cliff jumping," Jason noted.

"Peer pressure!"

Jason and Sabrina quickly asked a firefighter where the nearest cliff might be. He pointed out that they didn't have any cliffs nearby, but there were a few really large buildings that people commonly jumped from for fun. Again, it'd seem odd to others to have buildings built extra high strictly for jumping purposes, but here you have to entertain yourself somehow.

The building they chose wasn't particularly far from the collapsed structure they had just been playing in. Once inside, it took awhile for them to get to the top of the building because the elevators were in constant use. They weren't alone in their jumping endeavors. Four kids were riding the elevator with them, and they all talked about how lame the jump was. I doubt adding all four of their ages together would get close to my age. I'm in my fifties, for reference purposes only.

"I don't know, this building just doesn't compare to the one my parents took me to on my birthday," generic boy number one said, with his too-long blonde hair, rebellious clothes, and braces.

"I hear there is a building on the other side of the world that goes into space and that you get shot out of a canon!" generic boy number two piped in, apparently younger than the first. He sported brown hair, ripped clothes, and glasses.

"I would just get shot into space! That is the ultimate jump. Float on until you run into a planet," the only female in the group stated, looking the most tattered of the panel of kids. The boys listened well to the girl, as if having the most torn-up clothes showed great experience in performing ridiculous endeavors in this dimension.

"Yeah, that stuff is pansy compared to the jump my cousin made!" generic boy number three butted in. The other kids groaned.

"Your cousin didn't jump through a hole in the earth and come out the other side!" one of the other boys retorted as the elevator bell dinged, its doors opening.

I would continue writing out the argument if it were interesting. Just know there was a lot of heckling as the four made their way to the stairs that led to the roof. Jason and Sabrina followed a bit behind.

Upon exiting onto the roof, Jason noticed the wind had picked up. It sent a chill down his spine, which coupled with the fear of jumping from the roof. As each of the four kids jumped, the feeling of dread sunk deeper and deeper into his stomach. Jason wasn't sure what he was nervous about as he and Sabrina walked to the roof's edge. He couldn't die, so it didn't matter if he jumped.

"We should look for Leo," Jason said to Sabrina as Sabrina clapped excitedly, having just watched the full descent of each of the kids.

"You are right," Sabrina said as she moved closer to Jason. "We need to get down there first, though." Before Jason could process how she meant for them to get to the ground, Sabrina had grabbed his arm and dragged him off of the edge.

The fall was thrilling, scary, and quick to Jason. Multiple times in the descent, his emotions changed between anger at Sabrina for pulling him off the edge and excitement from free-falling. Jason let out a few screams of excitement, blinked, and then hit the ground. He had landed flat on his front on a patch of dirt. His body made an indention into the ground, over the indention of another jumper. He lifted his head up; it felt light and dazed.

"Ha! What a rush! How'd it feel to you Sabrina?" Jason asked as he carefully pushed himself to a sitting position. He then saw the oddest of sights. Sabrina was not crashed out on the ground as he had been but rather in the arms of a man in a green spandex suit with the letter L on it.

"You need to be more careful, young lady," Leo said to Sabrina, his teeth glistening as one would imagine a superhero's teeth to be. The children from earlier were also getting up from their indentions in the dirt. Jason couldn't help but notice Leo hadn't attempted to grab any of them. Leo hadn't even tried to get him either, and Jason fell at the same time as Sabrina.

"Careful? Where is the fun in that?" responded Sabrina with a grin as Leo slowly lowered her feet to the ground.

"Well, there aren't many beautiful ladies left in the world. I would hate to lose you."

"Beautiful? Really? Are we talking a seven or an eight?" Sabrina asked as she looked over her own body. Jason had, by this point, moved to Sabrina's side.

"I'd give you a B-plus," Jason said with a grin, looking at Sabrina.

"Not even the right scaling system," Sabrina responded, looking mildly offended.

"Mr. Leo?" Jason asked Leo.

"Yes, that is I. How do you know my name?" Leo asked Jason.

"Sabrina and I—I'm Jason, nice to meet you—are here to help you."

"Oh! So you and your girlfriend have come to help me bring justice to that woman?"

"Girlfriend?" Jason blurted out, snorting soon after.

"Boyfriend?" Sabrina too blurted out, having followed Jason's snort with one of her own. Would that be resnorted? "What would a B-plus have to do with a C-minus?"

Jason looked hurt after Sabrina compared his looks to a barely passing grade.

Both Sabrina and Jason took a few more moments to insult each other, but much like the children from earlier and these two kids now, I will skip writing it all out. Leo expelled a large breath of air before lifting his hands into the air, trying to get Sabrina and Jason to stop talking.

"All right! That is my fault for assuming. So you say you are here to help me? Good. I grabbed hold of the woman's ankle when she made the first jump using one of the DTPs back in my dimension.

The last time I saw this woman was around the burning building. I got sidetracked with helping all those poor people, so I lost her. What ideas do you two have?" Leo said to Sabrina and Jason, who had stopped arguing with each other. They both looked confused. "She had blonde hair, a slender frame, and kept giggling maniacally."

"Wait. You are chasing a woman? What for?" Jason asked Leo.

Leo shuffled uneasily for a few moments. He glanced around before motioning Jason and Sabrina to follow him behind a large trash bin. Once behind the bin, he began unzipping his spandex suit, much to the two's discomfort.

"Do not speak of what you see here."

"Of … of course not," Jason replied without being assured.

"My identity can be known by no other people. Do I have both of your words?"

Jason and Sabrina both nodded, Jason hoping that his identity was all that they'd see. Leo nodded back as he finished unzipping his outfit, pulling the top portion of his costume over his head, arms, and chest. It then flopped down at his waistline, revealing his muscular chest. His face was handsome as any might assume, with his well-defined jaw, beautiful blue eyes, and perfect hair.

Leo turned his right side to the incredibly enthralled duo and placed a finger on his well-defined triceps. There could be seen a very tiny hole, as if someone had jabbed him with a needle.

"There it is. She got me with a needle!"

I knew it; it was a needle. Just because I am writing the story doesn't mean I can't guess at what things are in it.

"So, some blonde-haired girl jabbed you with a needle? Why would she do that?" Jason asked as Leo put his spandex suit all the way back on.

"I am unaware, but we need to find her. Where do you think she went off to?"

Both Sabrina and Jason looked at each other, shrugging. It was true neither knew where she was, but both knew they were running out of time before they'd be returned to Jonas. So Jason motioned Sabrina to hand him the slip of paper and watch, which she reluctantly did, and he began to type in the dimensional code into the watch. Leo looked amazed.

"What are you calculating? The proper angle and velocity and which way she ran?! Genius!" Leo said with praise to Jason as he watched with enthusiasm as Jason finished typing in the numbers into the PDT.

"Yes. I'm calculating those things. Now, if you grab hold of an ankle—you too, Sabrina—we will use my calculations to teleport to where this lady has gone!" Jason said, lying through his teeth apparently.

He was slowly getting used to coping with alter-dimensional personalities. Their grasps on the world were far different than that of someone from a Control Dimension, so he figured he could make things up to follow along with what he thought was their ridiculous logic. Though how much less ridiculous is the thought of using a watch to transverse dimensions?

Sabrina begrudgingly plopped down onto the ground, perhaps still upset at being called Jason's girlfriend, and grabbed hold of Jason's ankle. Leo watched her do so before kneeling to the ground and wrapping an arm around Jason's other ankle.

"Though evil might try to escape the eyes of justice, they can never be unseen. For I …" Leo began a speech as Jason activated the calculator watch, causing the three to be pulled through dimensions, back to the Superhero Dimension. "Did I … did we just make a dimensional jump?" he questioned as he stood. "I felt the same way when I followed that girl. It was the same feeling of my body being strained as if it were being yanked through a tiny opening."

You see, I didn't lie about how it felt.

"This is my own dimension! She has returned here?!" Leo said as dramatically as one possibly could upon coming to his conclusion. "I will begin searching, starting by asking some of my superhero friends." He then thanked both Jason and Sabrina before heading off, telling them to activate his symbol on the giant spotlight when they found something out.

Jason waved as Leo ran off while Sabrina stood, folding her arms in front of her chest.

"They are so gullible. That is what I miss most about this dimension," Sabrina said with a heavy sigh. She then raised her shoulders and lowered her head before darting her eyes back and forth.

"Is everything all right?" Jason asked, turning to face her. She was wearing a black ski mask, black sweater, black gloves, black pants, and black boots. On her chest was the letter B. Does that stand for Bandit?

"Yeah …"

"You aren't worried that one of these superheroes is going to recognize you and lock you away, are you?" Jason replied, concern in his eyes.

"Maybe … This dimensional self of you looks like one of the ones I messed with."

Jason looked down and saw he was wearing blue spandex pants, red gloves, an orange shirt with a question mark on it, green shoes, and a top hat. I don't even want to begin to try to guess his superhero name.

"That doesn't surprise me," he responded, looking back up.

Sabrina got back on the ground, grabbing on to Jason's leg, sort of hiding her face.

"I've got a curious question," Jason asked Sabrina, looking down at her.

"If it is about me and this dimension, don't bother."

"No. It is about the watch. Why, after multiple jumps, are we pulled back to our starting dimension when the timer runs out?"

"What? How would I know? I'm sure Jonas has something to do with it."

Indeed, he does. It isn't anything too difficult to grasp. The watch usually returns to its home dimension when the timer goes off. Jonas just happened to override its home dimension using some of his dimensional voodoo. See how simple that is?

"Okay. I'll bug him then." He will do it.

The digits displayed on the watch slowly decreased until they reached zero. When they reached that point, both Jason and Sabrina were teleported back to the same single lamppost-lit area with the stairs.

After walking up the stairs, they were greeted by Teddy, who looked offended that he wasn't a part of the last adventure. Trandon was asleep. Sabrina picked up Teddy and proceeded to play with him while Jason went over to Jonas's room, being sure to knock first.

"Come in." Jonas's voice came from his chair, having just been awoken from a nap.

Jason filled Jonas in on the situation with Leo. Jonas promised to have Trandon search the dimensional logs. He said that Trandon might be slow, but if he wants his allowance, he will find the girl. Until then, Jonas said there was more work that Sabrina needed to get done, which Jason happily agreed to help with.

CHAPTER 10

———— ·❖· ————

The process of fixing the wrongs in the dimensions took a long time. So long, in fact, that Jason wasn't able to accomplish anything in his home dimension. Well, it isn't like he was accomplishing much before.

To prevent any more mishaps with his parents, Jason requested that before each task was given by Jonas, the dimensional personality who was sent to his dimension be placed as far from his home as possible. This also required Jason to determine a reason he wouldn't be around the house as often. He ended up taking Sabrina's advice and told his parents he was working at an adult video outlet. This kept them from wanting to visit him while on the job. Cara wasn't as upset anymore, because she finally got her license back upon turning eighteen. She rarely bugged Jason, at least with needing rides.

The Sabrina originally from Jason's dimension had been able to return in full. This was due to changes Jonas made where he allowed the other Sabrina to travel to and from. Jonas began using his Seer Dimension to keep Teddy and act as a relay point for Sabrina and Jason so they wouldn't have to keep disrupting other dimensions further. Seer Dimension is the name Jonas gave the dimension in which he stays.

Jonas had given the watch to Jason, knowing he would be more responsible, and gave Sabrina a ring with a small white opal on the top that would glow a brilliant white light whenever she was being summoned to another dimension. She mentioned that it was slightly demeaning, but whenever she saw the light flash and felt her finger buzz—oh that was another feature of it—that grin would creep across her face, and she'd press the opal to accept the summoning.

Jason had started to talk with the Sabrina he knew from his dimension again. She was the same as he remembered her being. Periodically, he'd catch her at Trendno, where, amazingly, she hadn't been fired from even after having missed a few days due to the Sabrina whom Jason had been traveling with.

Each time she was transferred due to her alter-dimension's hijinks, she traveled to the Evil-Plotters Dimension and explained it to Jason as the most incredible experience ever. A man there, who claimed to be her master, seemed to always be on the verge of some discovery or about to fall asleep. She said she never could quite tell. Either way, she got to spend the time there coming up with plots to destroy things or hold things hostage, and she'd never felt more alive in all her years of life. The only complaint she made was about some guy with a fragile left arm who stayed around there too. She said he mumbled too loudly. All of this made Jason worried about Sabrina to a slight degree because he wasn't sure if she'd try any of those evil plans in her workplace or, even worse, on him. He did his best to avoid the subject.

Jason's days became riddled with solving puzzles and other dimensional issues. He was given passcodes for his calculator watch to travel to the Seer Dimension and back home without having to worry about countdowns. Most of his time in the Seer Dimension was spent waiting around with Trandon and asking questions. Sabrina was only buzzed once Jonas was ready to send them on a mission. This was determined based on whether Jonas could sort things out enough to get them to the point of being fixable. If something ended up being beyond help, Jonas would skip it.

For example, there was an instance in which a whole tribe of musically inclined apes were transferred to a Control Dimension by some wild accident—an often-enough occurrence around here, especially for being an accident. The apes became a huge musical sensation and went on to sell multiple records. The problem in returning them to their proper dimension came when Jonas found out some had died from drug abuse, others died from obesity, and the remaining one went into exile at a zoo. They say you can still hear the ape pounding rhythmically on the bars of his cage.

Among the many things discussed between Jonas and Jason were a few questions Jason had that might answer some of yours. He asked about the watch and learned of its origins. The watch was made in his dimension, Control Dimension 05. The watch was designed to allow users to visit dimensions, not stay. When traveling, the watch's band wraps itself around the user to keep it from falling off the user's arm.

So how did Sabrina get hold of it then? Not on her own, I'll tell you that. Her master devised a technique of removing it from its owner's arm. He unbuckled it while the traveler wasn't paying attention. And by not paying attention, I mean he knocked the guy out, and by unbuckling it, I mean he shrunk the guy's arm using an evil invention and slid the watch off. The Evil-Plotter's Dimension's people are never up to any good, as you have thus far witnessed.

Jason was also curious about what Leo meant by the acronym DTP. He was too embarrassed at the time to ask and partly taken aback with what Leo said prior about Sabrina and him. Jonas explained that DTP is an acronym for Dimensional Travelers Point. These are links between dimensions that Jonas and Trandon monitor for traveling. They've been in place for longer than he can care to remember and are hidden. The only way to access one is by receiving a code from the Dimensional Travelers Alliance.

The Dimensional Travelers Alliance isn't quick in its responses either. The reason for the delay is that when using a DTP, your dimensional personalities don't swap places. Rather, they can coexist in one dimension, so a bit of thought has to go into DTP use to ensure the personalities are capable of coexisting.

"Did the Dimensional Travelers Alliance approve travel for the girl Leo was chasing?" Jason asked, interrupting Jonas's summing up.

"It is possible. Although, I haven't seen any displaced women that match the little description we have of her, so she must be using DTPs," Jonas responded.

"Could the Dimensional Travelers Alliance know?"

"I'd be embarrassed if they did! I'm the one monitoring the dimensions," Jonas replied, looking taken aback.

"Okay. So when Leo grabbed hold of the girl's ankle and traveled with her through the DTP, he retained all of his clothes. Now bear with me on this because it is hard for me to grasp." No surprise there. "When you said that even people from the Immortal Dimension sometimes don't exist, did you know that he didn't live in that dimension even though he used a DTP?"

Jonas looked at Jason for a few moments with a puzzled look. He then responded. "No idea. This job has made me a pessimist."

Anyway, let me resume my summing up. Jason did ask about how Sabrina was carrying that Statue of Liberty pen with her.

"You know the pen Sabrina was carrying with her?" Jason asked.

Quiet, Jason, I'm not done yet! Ahem. Jonas explained that small items could be taken with you when using a PDT; you just had to will it. Jason began putting things together and understood why Sabrina had been given all the slips of paper.

"Why didn't you tell me to will it?" Jason asked Jonas, as I give up on the summing up.

"Simple. I didn't think you'd be able to do it," Jonas replied, much to Jason's shock. "Oh, come on. You are still a baby in the eyes of dimensional travel. I couldn't expect you to understand how to will something with you." Jonas attempted to reason with Jason, but Jason was already offended. "Okay, the next jump I'll let you try it. Sabrina will coach you, and then you follow through."

Jason thought this was amicable.

The next task that Jonas assigned Sabrina was to apologize to the man whose arm her master had shrunk and taken the watch from. She was then required to return him to his own dimension. Jason followed along on this adventure because he felt it was only fair that he should get to bust into her bedroom as she had done his.

While in Sabrina's home dimension, they did end up visiting her apartment complex, but due to there being one of the daily threats upon the building, they didn't get to pay a visit inside. They instead met up with the shrunken-armed man, who was shopping for evil supplies within an evil supermarket. When asked if he wanted to leave, he opted to stay in the Evil-Plotters Dimension. He said he was growing attached to it ever since he realized he had a unique evildoer look going on. Plus it gave him a good backstory to explain why he was crazy—I mean, evil. He did longingly look at the watch on Jason's wrist, but he wasn't getting that back.

There were a few other instances where the correct personality of people had been swapped to wrong dimensions. In some cases, both people had opted to stay as they were and not return, but in the event of one person being disgruntled, both would be swapped regardless.

There were also a few stolen precious items that needed to be returned to their proper dimensions. This was the most difficult of tasks for Jason and Sabrina to face. This was because they were labeled as thieves when trying to return the items or when they attempted to take the thing back from whoever had originally stolen the item. At least Sabrina was decent at stealing. She didn't shrink anyone's arm, but she did plenty of punching.

When it came to the end of things, Jonas had one final task before he would let both of these individuals return to their regular lives without any more disruptions, save the nightmares. This task was the result of many hours of research on Trandon's part. This task had been on everyone's mind. Who stuck the needle in Leo's arm?

Sabrina appeared down near the lamp as usual and walked up the stairs to the main area. Trandon was visiting his mother, so Sabrina didn't look nearly as miserable as she usually was when there. Jason was discussing with Jonas miscellaneous sports teams, which neither of them knew much about; that seemed to be the subject of the conversation.

"Hey gals, what is going on?" Sabrina asked. Her attitude had been slowly falling further and further into a pool of distaste as she was becoming more and more trapped in her home dimension.

"Hmm, nothing more than the usual nothing," replied a fatigued Jason. He might have been tired because of the lack of regular sleeping hours or because his uncle was constantly pestering him for free rentals at his supposed workplace. Either way, he hugged Sabrina to bring Everyone-Is-on-Fire Dimension memories back. She just laughed and pushed him off. There was a lot of hugging going on in the Everyone-Is-on-Fire Dimension just so you know.

Jonas led them both over to the couch where Teddy had taken up residence. Teddy had grown so attached to the travelers that when they tried to leave him back in the Fantasy Dimension, he merely attached himself to Jason's ankle with claws drawn out and was ready to clamp down his teeth for extra support. Oh, and did I mention they found out he was male? If not so, then I'm telling you now that they did.

Teddy assumed his usual spot on Jason's shoulders as they all took seats on the couch. Jonas thumbed through images on the television with the remote until he located the point of interest. It was a blonde-haired woman dressed in boots and a loose blue dress who was dancing upon a grassy hilltop.

"There she is ... the woman who has been eluding us for quite some time. As pretty as she is, I'm surprised Trandon didn't find her sooner. It seems she has a broken PDT with her as well, but I'm unsure how she has made as many dimensional jumps as she has. I'd be careful," Jonas said, looking at Jason.

While Jonas talked to Jason, Sabrina took an extra-long look at the woman on the television as if in thought, probably disgusted by her attire. Jason, while drowning out Jonas's warnings, on the other hand, thought she looked incredibly similar to a lady from a certain musical film he was once forced to watch.

Jason and Sabrina had actually hunted down two other dimensional traveler objects—a bracelet and a stone that would dimensional jump at the command of thought but no longer worked. Jonas wanted to gather all of the PDTs that weren't currently in use or were in the hands of someone who didn't need them. He mentioned it was probably a safety hazard that not all of them were accounted for, but he had been too lazy to find them on his own. Also, they were the cause of most of the dimensional swapping that Sabrina and Jason had cleaned up.

"So we are clear on what must be done? Just return the PDT to me, and you'll no longer be required to run errands for me. Also, figure out what the woman's fetish is with poking people with needles or something. Regardless, after this, I will consider the debt repaid, Sabrina." Jonas gave her a big smile, but Sabrina let out a sigh as if she were tired of hearing about her debt. "All right. This is the Theme-Music Dimension, so try not to go insane with all the music in your ears."

Jason could hear from the speakers on the television a beautiful violin solo playing as they watched the woman. *Is that what he meant by Theme-Music Dimension?* Jason wondered. It wouldn't be the first, but hopefully, it would be the last weird dimension he traveled to.

"Here are the codes, Jason. Make it quick so I can send you back to normality! Also, my favorite show comes on in not too long, so vamoose." Jonas walked to his room to take a nap perhaps or maybe do some paperwork. Before he fully closed the door to his room, he turned to Jason and said, "Remember to be careful around this woman."

The words of caution from Jonas again bounced off of Jason's mind as he was trapped in it, thinking of returning back to the way things were. Normality sounded good to him. He was ready to stop the lies and resume life as a more mature man. He even figured he'd go back to college so he could finish his degree in English and pursue a real job of sorts. Maybe he could change to a technical degree or even get his doctorate. I think that is a little too ambitious for the moment, Jason—baby steps, please.

Sabrina sighed as she bent down and grabbed hold of Jason's ankle.

"You remember what I taught you about willing things with us?" Sabrina asked. "Just think really hard about what you need to go with you."

Jason nodded to her as Teddy crawled down and latched on to his other ankle.

"Don't worry. That PDT is coming back with us." Jason placed his hands on his hips after entering the numbers into the calculator watch and stood in that position briefly before saying, "Let's do this!"

Sabrina made an especially audible groan as Jason pressed the button on the watch. Teddy, Sabrina, and Jason were all pulled through the floor of the Seer Dimension, only to arrive upright in the Theme-Music Dimension.

Upon looking around, Jason realized they had arrived at a grassy open field with trees surrounding it. Jason smiled as he saw that he was dressed in brown pants, a white button-up shirt with suspenders, no shoes, clean-shaven, and his hair neatly tied behind his head.

Sabrina looked much less happy in her brown dress with large buttons, fluffy shoulders, and rough texture. It looked very similar in style to the woman's dress that they had seen on the television earlier. Teddy was dressed up as a miniature bear; no change there.

Jason took a step and heard music; it was uplifting and happy. Was his theme music going to be this good? Sabrina, on the other hand, had violins and tragic sounds fill the air around her, none of which seemed to cause a stir in her, except that she swatted the empty air a few times as if trying to hit an annoying fly. Teddy kept shaking around, as if attempting to trigger his music, but it seemed he wasn't granted a theme song. Instead, he chased a butterfly.

"Teddy, get that out of your mouth," Jason said in an extremely proper voice, a feature he and Sabrina had with these dimensional personalities.

Teddy obliged as he made a wretched face and rubbed his lips with a paw. I can only imagine what the bug might taste like, and from Teddy's reaction, it wasn't that grand.

Still enjoying himself, Jason discovered that as he moved quicker, the music quicken its pace to match. If he took a dramatic run, the music went along with it. If he looked sad, the music changed too. "Sabrina, this is great, isn't it?" Jason looked over at her with a hopeful smile. She darted her eyes at him quickly.

"Fantastic, if only I could get it to stop, it'd be better. Can we please complete this mission so I can think once again?" Sabrina's mouth had been gradually lowering at the edges into a frown of a grand magnitude. Quite possibly due to the sad violin solo that surrounded her, or was it the other way around? Which came first, the sad music or the frown? Let the philosophical ones sort that one out.

Jason didn't let her mood pull him down and instead tried other methods to get his tune to change—skipping, flailing his arms about, and falling onto the ground. I think that last one was supposed to be a cartwheel. After completing a few failed attempts of acrobatic grace, Jason caught up to Sabrina, who was walking toward a hill in the distance. It was similar to the one they saw the lady in the blue dress atop.

Sure enough, on top of the hill they saw a woman in a flowing blue dress with beautiful blonde hair. On the way up the hill, Jason spotted a rather sizable rock and stood upon it. He cleared his throat a few times to garner the attention of his dimensional companions. Once they took interest in him, Teddy in part because he was easily distracted by stupid things and Sabrina only because she probably wanted to be ready to laugh in case whatever Jason did hurt him, he spread his arms out to the side like a bird. Dramatic music began to play as he took pose upon the rock. Then the crowd hushed, except for Sabrina, who began questioning what he was doing. Jason leapt the full foot to the ground and landed with perfect balance. A fanfare sounded, and Teddy clapped.

"Good job, Jason. We'll sign you up for the Junior Rock Jumping League once we get done here," Sabrina said with a slight grin. Even when upset, that smile swept over her face with each sarcastic statement. Jason felt the sting of her insult. Not really, a bee just stung him, and dramatic violins played as Jason reacted.

After watching Jason nurse his wound and Teddy chase the bee for a good minute, Sabrina scoffed and returned to walking up the hill. Jason picked up Teddy and followed, complaining about how much his arm hurt from the sting.

When the trio got within talking distance of the woman, she turned to face them with a shocked look, as if she had caught someone spying on her while she was in the shower. The troubled look quickly turned into a smile, and she waved her hand in greeting. Jason and Teddy waved back. Sabrina just stared intensely, contracted her eyebrows, and tilted her head to the side.

"Hello there! Come to join me up upon this hill?" the lady asked. Her beautiful voice matched her beautiful face, both of which Jason had noticed. He smiled sheepishly as he walked toward her.

"I ... I ... I'm ... uh. I'm Jason," Jason stuttered out. The woman giggled and then looked at Teddy. "Oh, and this is Teddy." Teddy too seemed to be dumbfounded by her beauty.

"Charmed to meet such a handsome man and his bear. What brings you up to the top of this hill? Do you wish to dance with me?" Her smile lingered just enough to cause Jason's brain to lock.

"Well … I … yeah, yeah." I did mention Jason is a wordsmith, right?

"Enough chatting around." Sabrina pushed forward, knocking Jason out of the way. "Listen, lady, you pick up any weird dimensional traveling objects lately or cause grown superheroes to cry?"

The woman looked at Sabrina as if each word spoken by her were of a foreign language. She then rather gracefully stepped over to Jason and took both of his hands in hers, causing him to drop Teddy as she looked deep into his eyes. "Noble sir, what does this lady talk of? It is all gibberish to my ears!" Again, she flashed that smile.

"Look, it isn't the Medieval Dimension. You have a PDT on you, and we need it," Sabrina said.

The lady kept up her confused stare.

"Honestly. Just empty out your pockets, and we'll be done with this. We don't care about why you were poking that spandex dude." Sabrina paused for a moment. "Well, at least I don't care why."

"Empty out my pockets? That isn't something for a lady to do, especially one wearing a pocketless dress!" She smiled at Sabrina before returning her eyes toward Jason. "Poking a man? Can you believe her words?"

Sabrina scoffed, and her music turned sour as she walked back to the rock Jason had jumped off of earlier. She took a seat on it, looking back up the hill. The lady and Jason were both holding hands and frolicking about.

"I haven't introduced myself yet, my name is Amelia." The woman said to Jason as they were in midswing, music playing around them. Jason felt mixed feelings of excitement and lust. He was happy to be here but knew it was for the wrong reasons. Or did he know? I'm not sure if he is thinking at this point. "Oh, what a nifty object upon your wrist. Mind if I have a closer look?"

The lady took notice in the calculator watch and stopped their dancing. Jason looked down at it and then at her. He lifted his arm up for her to see it better. She then gasped in amazement and awe as he explained the features of the watch, including the digits and even dimensional travel, which made her laugh.

"Mind if I, if I try it on?" she asked.

The playful banter and music had loosened Jason up, making him feel nothing was wrong with this situation. He removed the watch from his wrist and slipped it onto her extended slender wrist. Teddy had crawled up Jason's body and onto his shoulders, peering down the whole time at the little event.

Amelia looked the watch over and admired it on her wrist. Sabrina yelled something out from behind them, and her footsteps could be heard running toward Jason.

Jason ignored Sabrina and watched as Amelia typed in a few random numbers. He then explained by pushing the plus symbol that it'd cause her to go into another dimension, assuming the digits entered were correct for that dimension. She looked up at him and batted her eyelashes.

"It isn't a plus symbol, idiot. It is a pound sign." Amelia's expression went from flirty to dirty in seconds. She grinned evilly and laughed before taking a few steps back.

Sabrina halted next to Jason, almost out of breath. "Give it back, Amelia!" she yelled between deep air intakes.

"Wait. How do you know her name?" Jason looked intrigued, seemingly unaware Amelia was stealing the watch. He must be in some trance from when she fluttered her eyelashes at him.

"It is too late! I am better, as always, Sabrina!" Amelia laughed as she quickly jabbed a needle into the side of the watch, similar to what Sabrina used to do. Cackling now, her finger then slipped onto the pound button on the watch, and she vanished from sight. Sabrina had made a lunge for Amelia but was far too slow to grasp her ankle in time.

"Are you two friends?" Jason asked.

Sabrina growled in anger as she stood back up. She stepped in front of Jason and slapped him hard enough that even Teddy reacted. What a drama bear.

"Stop your drooling! You just gave the watch to some stranger."

"Well, she wasn't a stranger. You knew her!" Jason responded, trying to put everything together while rubbing his blistering red cheek.

"The face and body I know from my dimension! I didn't realize the personality was the same too. I saw it on Jonas's television but didn't believe it then either. How could I have been so careless?!" Sabrina walked a few steps away from Jason, apparently frustrated.

"What do you mean you know her?"

"I'll explain later … Now, she had to get here somehow. There must be a Dimensional Travelers Point nearby. Look for something that might be out of place or that behaves strangely when interacted with." Sabrina took immediate control of the situation as if this were some sort of personal attack. It was, and there was about to be a girl fight going down in a dimension soon, I'm sure of this.

Sabrina grumbled as she frantically looked around. Jason got the brilliant idea to use Teddy as a tracking bear. Sabrina looked over at them as Jason flashed his hands, both riddled with the smell of lotion from Amelia's body, in front of Teddy's nose. Teddy was on the trail. He sniffed around on the ground like a dog, a koala bear dog.

Jason and Sabrina followed Teddy as he headed down the hill and then made a turn and went back up the hill. Teddy then made a drastic turn and started a more quickened pace down the other side of the hill and away from it. He led them so far away from the hill that Sabrina stopped following. Jason had gotten to the point where he was trying to catch Teddy so he could stop him from running wherever he was going.

Eventually, Teddy did stop once he located some fruit on a plant within a small thicket of trees. He was apparently no longer following the scent of Amelia, assuming he had been in the first place. Jason leaned on a nearby tree, out of breath. He wanted to start questioning Teddy's intentions on leading him out into the woods alone but instead breathed heavily. As he leaned on the tree, the most curious of things happened—it moved. Only an inch or so, but it moved, unsettling Jason's balance enough to cause him to take notice.

As he got off of the tree, it slowly moved back into the place where it was before. Jason leaned on it again, and sure enough, it moved slightly. He became amused with this and tried forcing the tree to go as far as possible by pushing it. After the tree had moved a good foot, it reached a branch down and slapped Jason on the back of the head. This caused Jason to stop pushing the tree. The tree returned to its original position once Jason had moved out of its way.

Sabrina came jogging up to them with one hand in her pocket, the other stretching out in front of her as she neared Jason. Jason put his arms up quickly to guard himself, not ready for a second handprint on his cheeks.

"Stop looking like an idiot. Did I just see this tree move?" She touched it with her free hand. Jason nodded. "Okay. Good job, Teddy. I didn't think you knew what you were doing. Now we need the code she put into the watch. You saw her type it in, Jason. Do you remember what she typed in?" She watched him think for only a moment before he shrugged.

"Nope. I was captivated by the fact that she didn't slap me."

"You didn't talk to her long enough." Sabrina pulled her hand out of her pocket, holding the needle she'd used on the watch between two fingers. Jonas had taken it from her due to not wanting her to cause more messes while they were trying to clean things up, but she somehow managed to steal it from him. I'd blame Trandon, that boy would do anything for her. "If we can just think what it is, I've got the tool to make us bypass whatever stupid restrictions that prevent us from following her."

"Wait. Why would we need that? Shouldn't Jonas just help us?"

"That old man? He sleeps more than my master back home. He is probably snoring right now and will only wake up when we start stomping around the dimensions," Sabrina retorted. She was probably right.

A few moments passed in silence. Jason stood with his mouth agape, still amazed that a tree could move. Sabrina turned the needle between her fingers while Teddy made noise, lifting his arms up toward Jason. Teddy's cries awoke Jason from his stupor, and he scooped down and picked up Teddy, thinking the cry for attention was just his desire to get back on Jason's shoulders.

After getting into Jason's arms, Teddy motioned toward Jason's wrist where the calculator watch used to be. He then began putting his fingers up in different combinations, as if representing different numbers. After a few iterations of the hand movements, Jason grasped what was going on.

"Hey, Sabrina. I think Teddy knows the code. Don't look at me like that. He was on my shoulders when she typed it in. It is possible. Bears have good memories. Teddy, do you know the code?"

Teddy nodded up at Jason while letting out a sigh as if relieved Jason finally caught on.

"What the … how can he even understand you? I mean, he never understood me when I wanted him to claw Trandon's face off!" Sabrina argued.

"Just … just go with it."

"If you think Teddy has that good of memory, then whatever." For a moment, she paused, rolling her eyes. "But you have to call the numbers out. That way, you look like the idiot, and I'll just be the one grabbing on to the idiot's ankle." Sabrina sat down next to Jason's legs and grabbed on to his ankle, mumbling small phrases of disbelief. She pressed her needle into the tree. Jason set Teddy down so that the bear could grab an ankle also.

"Wait. Before we do this, I have a question I want to ask you," Jason said, almost seeming to speak to the tree.

"Yes?" Sabrina responded.

She had to know the question was for her. Why would he be talking to a tree? Jason took a few moments to gather his thoughts.

"Why do we have to grab the ankle? I mean, why not an arm or something?"

Sabrina laughed. She laughed and laughed and laughed.

"I …" Sabrina laughed. "I thought it was going to be something sappy," Sabrina said, wiping away a tear. "Okay, I'm cool. It is because you travel feet first through dimensions. You don't see it, but it happens. If you grab any other part, you might get knocked off during traveling. It is quick, so it'd hurt to fall."

"So then we could use an arm?"

"Yeah, I guess so, but I'd stick with the ankles."

"What if you don't have ankles?"

"Well then … Jason! Teddy, show him what you saw, and let's get this over with." Sabrina's emotions are sporadic. Maybe Jason is to blame?

Jason pondered for a few moments before looking down at Teddy. He then watched as Teddy held up his paws, showing different sets of fingers that represented numbers. When he reached a number bigger than he had fingers (nine), he used his toes. At the resounding sound of Jason yelling out the last digit, the tree shook, the earth felt as if it were going to move, and then everything was still.

"It was worth a shot ..." Jason's voice trailed off as he felt as if he were being pulled through time and space again, his body only for a moment crunching inside out until he felt whole again.

In reality, the process is the same regardless of how you travel through dimensions. Your body is pulled feet first through the ground and out the other side to land feet first onto the dimension you are going to. It just feels very uncomfortable for those who are still unused to it. You have to wonder when Jason will stop collapsing to the ground.

CHAPTER 11

The trio took in their surroundings after a slight moment of recovery, or rather when Jason got off of the ground. Jason saw they were standing in a forest that was lacking trees. Well, there were trees actually, but most of them were flat on the ground as if they had been felled and left to rot.

Upon looking down at her lower body, Sabrina let out an audible sigh. "Great. I just can't escape looking ridiculous, can I?" she asked the air. Both Jason and she were still dressed the same as they were in the Theme-Music Dimension, voices included. Music no longer filled the air. I'm sure Sabrina is happy about that. Teddy still looked like a bear.

In the distance, they could see smoke and a few buildings, so they started walking that way. It was a city in the distance, but not the too distant range. Upon entering the city, they stopped. It was a shoddy-looking city with cracked brick walls on houses, bent lampposts, and people constantly looking over their shoulders. What happened to the upkeep here? The streets had potholes so large that people could fit in them. The few cars they saw each looked like a refrigerator had fallen on top of them. No building was bigger than two stories, and bricks and concrete littered the ground.

"Okay. If I know her, she'll be celebrating her victory somewhere. So we just have to find the closest party, and she'll be there, but finding a party might be very difficult given the state of this place. I recommend we split up," Sabrina said with many arm movements.

I think she wanted to split up so she could be the first to strangle the woman. Jason and Teddy nodded in agreement, and the three of them set off in different directions. Yes, Teddy went off on his own. I am not making this up.

The streets Jason walked on were scantily clad of people. Those who did brush past him looked nervous. Jason, on the other hand, looked like light shining in the gloom because of the size of the smile on his face.

After much walking through the depressing streets, he took to mind what Sabrina said about Amelia and entered the nearest bar. This was actually a difficult task for Jason because it looked like the closest bar was on either side of the street and directly in front of him. He decided to go with the one to his right because it still had four of its six windows intact.

Not unexpected, this place was packed full of the same looking sort from the street. Only difference was that these were drinking. Not to be left out, Jason went to the bar and ordered himself a cold alcoholic beverage. He took a seat on one of the barstools and glanced about the room. It was heavy with smoke and smelt of body odor mixed with alcohol, exactly as one would presume a bar to smell.

The lighting in the bar was as weak as one might imagine it to be, causing Jason to have a hard time seeing all of the patrons. Mostly he couldn't tell genders, so he stood up to walk around the bar and get closer looks. As he did, an arm reached around his shoulders and pulled him back down to his seat. It was a burly older man who must have led a physically labored life that dragged him back down to his bar seat. The man smelt very heavily of alcohol, almost as if it were his fragrance.

"Sit, son. There isn't anything better when it comes to curing the pain than a dozen drinks." The man motioned the barkeep over and ordered another drink for Jason, who had barely sipped through the one he was on. Truth be told, Jason wasn't the hugest fan of alcoholic beverages but rather likened to be part of the group. He should have listened more when they talked about peer pressure in high school, but he was being compelled to ignore the establishment at that point in time. Kids do that, right?

Seconds after ordering the drink, the man passed out, having not removed his arm from around Jason but rather using him for a pillow. As he uncomfortably sat there, Jason noticed a certain someone who sat a few seats from him. It was Amelia. His obliviousness knows few bounds. He tried to brush the burly man off but found his snoring mass to be nearly unmovable. Each deep breath and snort brought odors that no man should be forced to smell.

Jason eventually managed to weasel his way out from below the man's arm but ended up falling to the ground, and the man, who was using him as a pillow, followed. They both crashed to the floor with a thud that shook the foundation of the bar. In a regular place and time, this would've caused a stir, but here, the depressed faces and saggy eyes didn't lift from their drinks. Amelia was too busy making out with the random bar patron she was sitting beside to notice either.

After rather slowly getting out from under the burly man, Jason stood up and brushed himself off. He then moved over to Amelia; she was still making out with the other bar patron. Their drunken kisses looked very sloppy, and I'm pretty sure they were doing less making out and more slobbering on each other. Jason tapped Amelia on the shoulder. She didn't respond. Again, he touched her shoulder with a little bit more force, but no luck. So he did the most logical thing he could think to do, he pulled the barstool out from under her and sent her falling to the ground.

The guy she was making out with didn't like the sudden intrusion, so he punched Jason in the face, sending Jason flailing backward and onto the floor. The man then quickly disregarded Amelia's failed attempts at getting up and jumped to where Jason now lay, getting on top of him and pinning him to the ground. The man threatened Jason's life as he reared back his hand to unleash vast punishment for interrupting what was probably the only happy moment in his life.

With a great lunge, the burly man who had been using Jason as a pillow came to Jason's rescue as he pushed the other guy off of Jason and began a standard-issue bar fight. There were punches and tossing of people into wooden tables that broke upon contact. Jason breathed a sigh of relief and used one of his hands to feel all over his face. He was bleeding from his nose and lip, but nothing was broken. Truth be told, he didn't exactly know how a broken nose felt. All he knew for sure was that something seemed broken on his face. He then stood up and moved over to Amelia, nodding at the burly man who was midfight. Amelia was now on her knees, downing drinks and looking pretty drunk.

"Oh, oh. Hey there, Jackson!" she said with a slur, trying to stand to greet him. Instead, she put on a pouty face, realizing she was unable to stand up. "I seem to have misplaced my barstool. What … what brings you to this ol' place? Ya miss me?" She grinned real big. She wore the same blue dress she had on from the other dimension but looked less miserable than Sabrina while wearing it. Jason smiled down at her before snapping back to reality and remembering the mission.

"You took my watch, and I am here to get it back," Jason stated as he reached his hand out.

Amelia took his hand and used it to assist her in getting up. She leaned her body up against his and chuckled before removing the watch and handing it over. Jason looked over at her, shocked that she had handed the watch over so quickly. He then strapped it back onto his wrist.

"Disappointing, Jacky boy. I thought you had come to see me!" She teased him by licking her lips before wobbling back to a bar seat and clumsily sitting down. "But who really wants that, right? My own sister wanted to leave so badly that she promised to bring back some amazing item. I haven't seen it!"

"Your sister?" Jason asked. He had gathered that Sabrina knew Amelia well but didn't realize it was that well. He honestly should've put this together by now.

"Yeah, the dark-haired moody one is my sister," Amelia responded.

Amelia tried to grab a glass of alcohol but failed to, spilling the contents onto the bar. This annoyed the barkeep who had already been cleaning up a mess of hers from earlier. She just winked at him, or at least I think that was a wink—she kind of half closed one eye and fully the other.

A great battle raged on behind Jason as a few more patrons in the bar had begun fighting for little reason other than a broken table or spilled alcoholic beverage. He looked back up from the watch, having tested it to ensure it wasn't broken, and saw through the smoky haze that Amelia was now making out with the bartender. Jason moved quickly over to where they were making out and tapped the bartender on the shoulder.

"Excuse me, sir," Jason said.

The bartender didn't answer and instead pushed Jason away with his free arm.

Something clicked inside of Jason's head. He was tired of being drug along. He was tired of being told what to do. He was tired of being pushed around. So he did something that seemed logical at the time. Jason punched the bartender in the face, watching as the man toppled over dramatically and fell to the floor. All right, that wasn't that hard of a punch. Have you seen Jason's arms? Amelia looked at Jason, perhaps confused as to why he got rid of another one of her kissing partners.

"Let me get you something to drink," Jason said, shaking his hand before reaching across the bar. He poured a glass of water from the faucet and handed it to Amelia. She looked at him as curiously as a drunk can look at someone.

"I really do think you are cute, John Johnny John John," Amelia slurred out, drinking large heaps of her alcohol-free drink. Jason also poured himself some water, wanting to rid himself of the massive headache he was now suffering from the punch he'd taken earlier. Amelia leaned over and tried to kiss Jason, but he moved out of the way, so she instead rustled his hair with her hand.

"So why'd you take it then? The watch, that is," Jason asked, wanting to get to the point and get this awkward time over with. Plus he wanted to do anything to keep her lips moving and not on someone else's.

"Well …" Amelia leaned in and caught Jason's lips off guard. She locked them in a kiss that could last days.

"You hussy!" Sabrina said from the entrance to the bar. She then stormed through the fighting patrons, pushing a few out of her way. She looked at Jason and then at Amelia. "I expected this from you, Amelia, so no name-calling is in order."

Amelia and Jason's multiday kiss had been broken up, which was good for Jason, seeing as the taste on her lips was horrid.

"Hey, Sister," Amelia said as she flopped off of the barstool. They circled each other, dramatic camera angles everywhere, their eyes locked in contempt. A quick close-up of Jason looking shocked that he was called a hussy, and then the camera would roll out to a panoramic view of the practically toppled over bar if there were one.

"Stepsister, where is the watch?" Sabrina asked.

By now they had made a few circles. Amelia lifted up her wrist as she ran into the bar. She groaned a bit before lazily checking each wrist for the watch and then shrugging. Jason sighed and held up his arm with the watch on it.

"Oh yeah, Jeff. I gave it to you, honey. Mmm … how about some sugar to go with your honey?" Amelia leaned over to kiss him but tripped and ended up in Jason's arms.

Sabrina looked annoyed but let out a sigh of relief. She then assisted her sister to a barstool and sat beside her. Jason took a seat next to Amelia too. Sabrina then grabbed one of the many pitchers of alcohol and poured some into a glass, drinking a bit after doing so. They sat there for a few moments in silence.

"You have to admit the Theme-Music Dimension was kind of fun, guys. I actually didn't think you could handle it, Sabrina," Amelia stated, searching around for something else to drink besides the glass of water that Jason kept filled for her. "You know what I bet your theme music was, Sab-a-rinia?" She paused for a few seconds as if awaiting a response. "I'm a loser. I'm a loser. Look at me. I'm such a loser!" Amelia busted into laughter as she leaned far over into Sabrina's personal space and somehow made it back up with an audible sound of excitement. Jason even had a laugh at that one, but he received a heaping dose of evil-eye from Sabrina and stopped.

"So what was the point of this? Take the watch from our resident idiot and then leave us there?" Sabrina asked Amelia. (The resident idiot was Jason, of course.) "And what of the spandex dude?"

"Spandex dude? Oh, that hunky man? I dunno. I just thought he was cute. Girls like a little chase now and again," Amelia said with a giggle. Then, after a brief pause, as if calculating what Sabrina said in her head, she added, "And don't call my man an idiot. Why, he's so smart he tricked me into giving him back the watch! But you know I would've come back for you guys … after a few drinks, of course."

Amelia's words made Jason smile a bit even though he began to realize she was just out having fun and messing with people.

"Besides, you stole it the first time and wouldn't stop bragging," Amelia noted. "I just wanted you to see how it felt to be on the losing end."

At this point, heartfelt music would be played, which would annoy Sabrina to no end if they were still in the Theme-Music Dimension.

"Okay, just stop crying. What dimension are we in?" Sabrina patted her crying stepsister on the back. Amelia had broken out into tears after spilling the last alcoholic drink that was in reaching distance of her.

"I'm … not quite sure. I entered a random dimensional code and used my Dimensional Device Disruptor to get here." Amelia motioned over to a martini glass that held her needle in it.

Sabrina looked shocked as her eyes gazed upon the martini glass. She then questioned her stepsister as to why she would do that to her Dimensional Device Disruptor.

"They were out of umbrellas, so I needed something to give my drink pizzazz. Also, I might have ruined the needle and made the drink taste funny."

Jason shook his head. "Do you have any other tricks up your sleeve?"

Amelia looked at Jason and grinned.

"I dunno. You can frisk me if you'd like," she said, moving toward Jason. Jason stood up and sidestepped Amelia. He then stood behind Sabrina, placing an arm on her shoulder as if trying to use her for a shield. "You were all into me a few minutes ago. What happened, Josh?" Somehow in her drunken stupor, Amelia noticed Jason's hand on Sabrina's shoulder. "Are you dating my sister?"

"What?" Jason and Sabrina simultaneously said before fumbling over excuses as they stepped away from each other. I'm uncertain what they are doing. All I know is Jason has kissed both of them, so he'll be the one to explain it I'm sure.

As Sabrina and Jason kept muttering back and forth, Amelia pulled a retainer out of her mouth, causing the duo to stop talking and look at her.

"What is that?" Sabrina asked.

"It is a worthless PDT," Amelia responded with a pouty face. "It doesn't even work anymore. Well, I mean it does work because it keeps my teeth in line, but it won't let me dimensional travel."

Both Jason and Sabrina made a face of pure displeasure at the sight of the retainer. Sabrina grabbed an empty glass, holding it under Amelia's outstretched hand and let her drop the retainer into the glass.

"Well, that was unexpected. Let's go," Sabrina stated, thumping the bar counter with her finger. She then looked down into the glass cup she held as if analyzing the retainer inside of it. "Where is Teddy?" She looked up after asking, eyes squinted.

"Teddy? Do you mean that adorable bear? I want to squeeze 'im and stuff 'im full of stuffing," Amelia proclaimed to wide-eyed stares from both Sabrina and Jason. "What? What are we looking at?" She glanced behind her and to the sides.

Sabrina shook her head before turning toward the exit to the bar and walking. Jason went over to the unconscious barkeep, apparently having been concerned the whole time they were there. He checked the man's pulse and let out a deep sigh, realizing his incredible punch didn't kill the man. I call it an amazing punch because it was unbelievable that he actually hurt someone with it. Jason and Amelia then headed out of the bar, following Sabrina.

Outside, things were as run-down as they had been prior to Jason entering the bar. As they walked down the street, they saw the usual sort of people one might see in this dimension. These people looked disdained and broken. It was rather depressing really.

"So this is your sister then?" Jason asked Sabrina, having briefly caught her eyes with his.

"Stepsister. No resemblance, can't you see?" Sabrina said, smiling next to Amelia, who smiled as well. "Let's find Teddy."

As they walked down a street nearly barren of life, a siren sounded, and the few people who were on the street started to run and scream. Their arms flailed about in unison as if they had practiced this a hundred times. As Sabrina, Jason, and Amelia stood there staring at the chaotic mess around them, something crept up, something big. The ground shook as it crept nearer. Birds scattered, trees broke, and the few buildings that still stood lost their courage to hold together and began to crumble.

Jason was the first to turn and see it, and he was the first to let out a scream. He saw a giant furry creature jump toward them. It had wide-open eyes, a sniffing nose, and massive ears. Oh no, it was a giant rabbit! Each time it landed from a jump, the ground shook. Its feet were as long as a car and its cute little nose wiggled such a wind current that it could knock a man down.

It wasn't alone. There were others, and they all looked hungry. Jason felt for a moment like the weight of the world was on his shoulders—after his scared scream, of course. He thought that he would muster the strength, take up a fallen weapon, and slay these beasts for the benefit of this world. He glanced about and didn't see a fallen weapon, so he instead resorted to plan B, which involved running and flailing his arms about. Honestly, it is the best thing he can do in this situation.

The three of them sprinted through the streets, with Jason at the lead. Amelia almost didn't follow at first because she seemed too interested in petting a giant rabbit. It wasn't until Sabrina yelled out her name that she followed, muttering something to the rabbit along the lines of, "Sorry, I got to go. My sister is mean."

Jason was unsure if they were being followed by the rabbits, watched, or neither. The giant rabbits just hopped around the town, landing on buildings and cars alike. He was unaware of their purpose, and I'm sure he didn't want to find out.

Quickly, the trio located a less-than-crumbled building with a closed door. Jason took a few steps back and sprinted forward in an attempt to bust down the door but was powerfully rejected. He leaned on the door for a second, holding his arm while complaining about the door being made of iron or something.

Sabrina stepped up and pushed him aside. She then opened the door using the doorknob, eying him in the process. Once inside, they came to a rest, sitting on the floor against the wall of what seemed to be someone's house. No matter, they were safe. Amelia stumbled over to a couch and located a television remote. She then proceeded to turn on the television.

"What are you doing?!" Jason whisper-yelled out. "They will hear you. I'm pretty sure of it. I mean, they've got ears the length of a semitruck!" He became nervous, and whatever testosterone he had built up from punching the bartender had faded now at the sight of giant rabbits.

Amelia ignored him and just turned the volume up. Some food show was on, and she looked hungry. Sabrina rolled her eyes at Jason and joined Amelia on the couch. She picked up a bag of chips that was next to her. She and her stepsister partook in consuming them.

Jason looked around the room, which looked recently abandoned. There were fresh drinks on end tables, the bag of chips Amelia and Sabrina were eating from, and clothes draped on the back of the couch that looked ready to be tucked away into a dresser drawer. Jason started to loosen up until the point he swore he heard something falling. It sounded as if someone had dropped an object from an incredible height. Was it on the television? Nope, they are cooking pizza, which looks delicious. Okay, what could be falling? There could be more rabbit overlords; the ground is still periodically shaking.

Great. That is all we need—more furry butts to avoid getting sat on by, Jason thought. He then stood up and looked out the nearby window, trying to be covert as to avoid being seen by a surely bloodthirsty rabbit. The falling sound kept getting louder.

With a crash, the roof over where the television sat caved in, and a large object landed on top of it, just feet from where Sabrina and Amelia sat. It was orange, sizable, and made a mess of the room. Jason moved over to it, shielding his eyes from the floating dirt and debris. As he got close to it, the ground shook violently as a rabbit landed on the other side. It looked down at him with enormous eyes before quickly gnawing on the orange object, pieces of it falling about.

Amelia moved in closer and reached down to grab a piece of the orange object. She slowly moved it up to her mouth, almost missing at first but somehow landing home and began chewing. Sabrina and

Jason watched her intensely, but neither should be surprised of the drunk.

"It tastes … it tastes like orange," Amelia said as her eyes squinted, obviously in deep thought.

"You mean like *an* orange," Sabrina replied as pieces from the rabbit's rabid chewing landed in her hair. She inched farther away from the orange object and giant furry critter.

Amelia shook her head as she munched. "Well, to me it looks like a giant carrot. How about that? Does it taste like one of those?" Amelia snapped her finger and pointed at Sabrina, signifying that was the correct thing she was trying to say.

"How many drinks did you have, hon?" Sabrina asked her stepsister.

Amelia stretched her arms out real wide and grinned.

"Ah, makes sense," Sabrina noted, "now come along and leave the nice rabbit to its feast."

Amelia waved to the rabbit as they both walked toward the room's exit. Jason had finally stopped staring, relieved that they weren't the rabbit's chosen feast. Sabrina grabbed his arm and walked him out of the door along with her stepsister. It isn't every day when you get to cross into a dimension where rabbit overlords require a feast of carrots that are dropped from planes. Maybe it isn't every lifetime. Unless you live in this dimension, in which case I apologize. Not for what I said but for the fact that you live here.

Up in the sky, they saw the remnants of the last planes flying away. Multiple locations around the city had carrot landings. Each landing had rabbits sitting around and gnawing on the recently dropped carrot. In all, there must have been a few dozen of these sizable beasts, chewing and thumping their way to happiness.

Amelia tried multiple times to pet the rabbits but was always being pulled back by her stepsister. I'm sure Sabrina contemplated being a single child at one point, but there is a bond between siblings that is stronger than being devoured by a rabbit. The trio had resumed their search for Teddy.

After walking a few more minutes, they saw Teddy. He was plopped on the street, enjoying some carrot with a rabbit. He smiled and waved as they came near. Amelia took a seat next to Teddy and proceeded to bask in his fur. Teddy smiled at all the attention and shared his carrot pieces with her.

"Well, at least they are happy. Are we ready to go, Jason?" Sabrina asked. Her eyes were dull with enthusiasm for their situation.

Amelia looked up at Sabrina. "Sabby-tabby, you got something blinking in your pocket." Sure enough, something in her pocket was blinking, and I'm surprised that the drunk was the first to notice. Sabrina pulled the blinking opal ring from her pocket, smirked at it briefly, and then slid it onto one her fingers.

"It looks like Jonas agrees," she noted. "Grab hold, gang. Bring the food with you, Teddy." Teddy held a few pieces of carrot in one hand and wrapped the other around Sabrina's leg, and Amelia followed suit. "Well, I've got these two. You good, Jason?"

He nodded as he typed in a bunch of random digits into the watch. Jonas had told him to use the watch once they were done, and it'd return him regardless of whatever digits he entered. He could wait for the countdown to end, but there were a few hours left on the watch. Apparently, Amelia hadn't planned on returning to Jason and Sabrina anytime soon.

Sabrina pressed the opal on her ring, and they were gone. Jason lingered for a moment, breathing in the sweet smell of carrot. They did it. It had taken months, but they were done. He could be normal now. But what was normality? When was Sabrina going to exact revenge on him for kissing her stepsister? Why would she care anyway? It wasn't his fault. Jason's head was littered with all these thoughts, but he just shook them away and pressed the worn-away pound sign.

CHAPTER 12

————— ⊛ —————

Jason felt that the darkness surrounding him was more than it had ever been before. *Where was that darn lamp? Maybe Jonas forgot to pay the electric bill. Whom would he pay the bill to anyway?* Jason thought as he reached out his hands, not touching anything but cool air.

"Sabrina? Amelia? Teddy?" He spoke to the darkness as he shuffled his feet around. While scuffling his feet along the floor, he eventually hit something stone that stood erect, sort of where he would have guessed the middle of the room would be. It was a sizable object, only a foot shorter than him, and had a flat surface on the top. Jason leaned his arms on it and stood there, looking into the utter darkness.

"Testing, testing, one two three. Can you hear me?" A voice came from seemingly nowhere in the room. Jason turned his head from side to side as if trying to see who was talking to him. "A yes or no answer would suffice."

"Yes, I can hear you," Jason replied to the darkness, thinking Jonas was playing a joke on him. He grinned and kidded around a bit. "But you are getting a little feedback from your speakers. Might want to turn the volume down."

"Speakers? What speakers? This is my voice! It is all natural and booming directly into your ears!"

"Sure it is, Jonas. Sure it is …" Jason replied, feeling the stone object he had his arms on. As he did so, he realized the stone object felt more and more like a podium. In fact, he'd bet on it.

"Jonas?" the voice questioned. "Oh, you mean the older man who watches the Seer Television for us. This is not him."

"Right. You landed me in the Darkness Dimension in some room with a podium. Let me guess. I'm naked too!" Jason really was going far-fetched here. He then checked his chest and legs with his hands, noticing he was clothed. "Okay, well you at least set me in front of a podium."

"He is right. You are a bit odd." A brilliant light appeared in front of Jason, causing him to shield his face with his arms. Before him, a rather short female appeared with her arms crossed, sitting on a very comfortable-looking red velvet chair. Her dark-black hair was lined with silver strands, all neatly tucked into a bun behind her head. Her face looked of average age with a few wear lines. She wore what looked to be a gray exercise suit. The lady looked Jason over as if she hadn't seen him before. "He did recommend you."

"Recommend me for what? Is this some kind of joke?" Jason was used to being the center of practical jokes and figured a lady who magically appeared in an empty room would not be honest. The woman shook her head but said nothing. She then picked up a sheet of paper that was wedged between her and the armrest of the velvet chair she sat in. After spending a few moments looking at it, she lifted the document above her head.

Nothing happened for some time, making Jason feel a little awkward. The lady cleared her throat, which made Jason start to walk out from behind the podium. She then lifted up her other hand and placed it flat out, signifying him to stop.

"Give me a second. There are small benefits to being me, even if they don't work all the time and even if my voice does sound like a man's," the lady stated, seemingly growing impatient at something.

Jason shifted nervously, having just realized he was the one who had accused her of sounding like a man. The lady's patience wouldn't have to be stretched any further as the paper left her hand and landed on the podium in front of Jason in a flash.

"See? It only takes twenty or so seconds before things start to work around here."

Jason reached his hand down and lifted up the sheet of paper. As he did so, a light came from above him, allowing him to see the words typed on the paper.

"Employment application? What is it for?" Jason asked after reading the top line of the sheet of paper. He then looked at the lady.

"Keep reading …"

Jason gave her a squinted, confused stare before looking back down at the paper. He read aloud. "FOR THE POSITION OF DIMENSIONAL WARDEN." Below this was a paragraph of text and below that was a line for a signature, another for dimension, and one for the date. He started to read the article but was interrupted by the lady's voice.

"The position of Dimensional Warden has recently been reopened, mostly due to the ill fate that beheld the last warden. We would like to offer this position to you. The Dimensional Warden's job is both taxing on the body and mind. It'll require you to be able to handle any and all dimensions that we send you to. In the event you feel you are no longer able to fulfill your duties as Dimensional Warden, we reserve the right to berate you until you man up and do them. These duties include, but are not limited to, returning lost Dimensional Travelers to their proper dimensions, seeking out and repairing Dimensional Transportation Devices, being an errand boy, and whatever else your boss's boss sees fit to assign you to do. By signing below, you agree to do these duties."

The lady completed her lengthy statement just as Jason's eyes had finished tracing through the paragraph. They matched up perfectly. She then looked him in the eyes with a smile.

"I typed that up just a few minutes ago, and it is still fresh in my mind," she said as Jason looked at her, amazed that she was able to recite it word for word. "There is a nominal pay in your home dimensional currency, and all expenses will be covered for other dimensions."

Jason stood in silent, deep thought.

After a few moments of silence, the lady spoke up, her voice sounding frustrated. "What is it? Don't you want this job?"

"I do, ma'am. It's just that there is one problem." Jason looked up from his thought process in a dramatic way.

"And that is?" the lady responded with a lengthy hold on the last word, tilting her head a little at the same time.

"I need a pen to sign this form with." Jason made a motion with his hand that was similar to writing. The lady smiled and lifted her hand again. After a few moments of waiting, she began to look agitated and mumbled something about someone needing to do his job. As Jason blankly stared out into the emptiness, he heard a loud clank upon the podium before him and felt something hit his chest. It was a pen, a Statue of Liberty souvenir pen. Jason took a look at it and recognized it as the one that Sabrina had stolen even though it probably looked no different than any other Statue of Liberty souvenir pen. He then pulled off the base of the statue, which revealed the tip of the pen.

"Jonas gave that to me. He said he found it in his trash can. So sweet of him," the lady said before pressing her lips together.

Jason signed and dated the paper and then wrote in his dimension: Control Dimension 05. After writing all of this down, he decided to test whatever it was that the lady had been doing and lifted the paper above his head. Within moments, something snatched it from his fingers and landed the paper neatly in the lady's lap. She quickly looked over the paper.

"Good. It is settled then." She stood up. "My name is Velma, and I'm your boss's boss." She outstretched a hand toward Jason. He just stood there for a few minutes as if waiting for something to happen. "You'll have to come here, dear. There isn't anything magical that will move our hands closer to each other."

"Oh, sorry," Jason said as he walked to the lady and shook her hand, noticing that as he got closer to her that he really didn't see any more of the place they were in. "Nice to meet you."

"You too, dear. Now, do you have any questions? You did seem to be in some minor trance there for a minute. It made me think that you weren't going to accept the job offer." Velma lifted her hand up with the paper in it, and within seconds, the paper was gone.

"I was in total shock. This is like a dream. Only real, I think." Jason started rambling.

Velma reached out and pinched the blabbering Jason. He recoiled with a slight look of pain.

"You felt that. You aren't dreaming," she stated. She then noticed the watch on his arm. "Oh, and you'll be getting an upgrade to that." She lifted her hand again.

A hummingbird came crashing down not too far to the side of Jason, a package held in its beak. "So, you found out about my secret courier," Velma said to Jason as the little bird lifted itself up, leaving the package on the floor. "Aren't you going to give that to him?"

"Lady, I brought the package from like two feet behind you to here. Isn't that enough? Geez." The hummingbird responded, much to Jason's amazement. He then watched as the bird flew off into the darkness.

"He was returned by one of our wardens while his was on a trip to the Fantasy Dimension. I believe you've been there. The poor thing kept begging me for a job because he didn't want to return to his dimension and sing anymore love songs. So, I put him to work."

Jason bent down and picked up the package, while Velma tried to convince herself that the hummingbird was worth keeping. He then untied a string that wrapped around the small box and opened it. Inside the package was a similar watch to his in shape but with no visible buttons. The band on it was made of metal, and the whole thing was black.

"Another PDT?" Jason looked at Velma, understanding that he probably needed a way to travel for his job but was unsure why he needed another one.

"Yes, a new one, in fact! Upgraded and more reliable. You are our guinea pig."

Jason removed the old watch from his wrist and handed it to Velma's outstretched hand. He then put on the new watch and looked down at it.

"Just tap the screen," she directed.

Jason did so, and the screen lit up with a blue light. The screen was blank. After a few seconds of inactivity, the light faded into a dimmer blue light with the time showing on it.

"It'll do that after a little while."

"This is incredibly neat, and it looks so cool, but how do I enter a dimensional code to travel?" Jason asked as he looked at the watch, periodically tapping the screen to see it light up.

"Of course it looks cool. Couldn't have you out of fashion, now could we?" Velma replied. "Well, for traveling, you'll have to use your mind. Similar to how you would use it to pull things with you through dimensions. Once the screen is lit, you just think the dimension you want to go to, and it'll display it on the screen. From there, you can tap it once, and you'll be off. Similarly, Jonas can send you requests, and it'll display the dimension he is summoning you to. From there, you tap the screen, and you are off!"

Jason looked down at the watch, feeling awed at the incredible upgrade to the old watch. A few of the keys were beginning to stick on it.

"The best part about this watch is that it doesn't behave as that old watch. You can enter dimensions without disrupting the current dimensional self at all," Velma continued as Jason kept messing around with the watch.

"What do you mean?"

"You won't swap dimensional places anymore, dear."

"I always thought that was a major flaw of the watch."

"It isn't a major flaw. It is as designed. We can find multiple personalities in a single dimension pretty easily but finding a swapped character can get tricky." Velma licked her thumb and then rubbed it on her chair as if she were trying to remove a stain. "I hear that girl you had with you had further circumvented our security measures with her needle."

Jason nodded. I'm surprised, he looks to have understood what she said. He then saw the screen on the watch light up. He read the words that appeared on it aloud, "Seer Dimension. I guess he is already calling me back," Jason said, looking at Velma.

"Good. It is time for you to get to work then. Make me proud." Velma started to fade from sight as she sat back down. "Oh, I want that pen back. It does actually write rather well."

Jason mindlessly handed the pen over to her slightly faded hand. Velma thanked him and continued to disappear until all that was left in the room was Jason. Well, minus the light that cast down on the podium, but then it too dimmed. And then Jason was standing there, truly alone.

"Totally awesome," he said with a huge grin as he tapped the lit watch, waiting for a moment after doing so. He then tapped it again;

yet, nothing happened. "Ha! This is too funny, Velma, too funny." Jason lowered his head and closed his eyes, thinking of being isolated in this darkness for eternity. He then opened them to the feeling of light beating on his eyelids and saw before him the lamppost from the Seer Dimension. "Oh, perhaps you weren't joking then." Had they improved the dimensional travel? He hardly noticed being pulled through the floor.

Jason walked to the stairs and went up them. At the top, he saw the group crowded around the couch. They were watching and laughing at the Seer Television. Teddy was the first to notice Jason entering the room and promptly ran over to hug his ankle. Sabrina got up from the couch, pushing her stepsister's sleepy head from her shoulder, and walked toward Jason. She noticed the brand-new watch on his wrist almost immediately.

"Cool watch. Where'd you get it?" she asked with a slight grin.

Jonas brushed past her and grabbed Jason's arm. He then used his foot to push Teddy off of Jason's leg before guiding Jason into his room.

"It is good to have you on board!" he said once they were not too far in the doorway.

"So you already know?"

"Of course. We were watching you on the television! What do you think we were laughing at?" Jonas said. He pulled the old calculator watch out of his pocket. "Just got dropped off by a ticked-off hummingbird seconds before you arrived. Let me set it in its proper place."

Jonas turned his back to Jason and was now facing a shelf that was taller than the both of them. It had sectioned off squares that held miscellaneous objects in them. Most of it looked to be random junk that he had collected, much like the rest of his room. The only interesting objects to Jason were two rows full of PDTs. Jonas placed the watch in its slot in the far-right box and then took the time to explain to Jason the different PDTs.

In the top-left box there lay a bracelet. The bracelet was adorned with trinkets that each hung from its silver beaded band. Each one of the trinkets was a different color and a different object—a blue peace sign, a green palm tree, a yellow happy face, a red anchor, and a black ninja star. The last two didn't seem to fit into the theme the bracelet had going on, except that the creator of this object was a fan of ninjas and pirates. It requires dancing to activate the dimension jumps with the bracelet, a reason it is considered useless because nobody but the creator knows the dance moves, and if anyone else knows them, I'm sure they don't want to perform them in public.

To the right of the bracelet, lying in an adjacent box, sat a stone. The stone was a glossy, cloudy stone that was extremely smooth to the touch and would easily fit in a grown man's hand. Originally it was clear, but due to a frustrating toss by its creator for taking him to the Amazonian Dimension by accident, it has lost its ability to work, as did the creator upon being knocked silly by very tough-looking women. When a person thinks the dimension he wishes to travel to while squeezing the stone in hand, it clouds up and takes him to the desired dimension. In case you are curious, the creator of the stone wanted to go to the Amazing Dimension. Guess the stone didn't fully understand his mind's accent.

Next in line lay the ring that was designed by Jonas for his son, Trandon, and used briefly by Sabrina. Its golden band looked beautiful as it wrapped around the base of the white opal that lay on top of it. The opal would flash a bright light whenever someone was trying to call the wearer back to the Seer Dimension. Jason witnessed Jonas performing the task of summoning the ring wearer back a few times. Jonas would walk down to the lamppost and place his hand on it. He then would say, "Return, or be late for dinner," and walk back to his office. Not too long after saying the words, the one wearing the ring would show up in a corner of the lower room. Jonas explained the phrase was suggested by his wife, mostly because that is what she said to him all the time.

In the lower-left-hand box, sat the retainer. It was created by a woman who wanted a quick escape from crazy men when in other dimensions. This was not created by Amelia but rather someone else, which would've been a good guess. As one might know, saliva doesn't mix too well with electrical objects. This caused the retainer to shock its creator one too many times, which happened to be twenty-three times. Amelia came into possession of it after witnessing the final failure and promised that she'd give the woman the watch her sister stole if she could have the retainer. This exchange hasn't happened, of course, and the creator of the retainer probably doesn't really care to this day. She more than likely just wants her mouth to stop feeling numb.

Amelia's Dimensional Device Disruptor was stored here also, broken after the incident with her martini. Alongside it in a locked glass container was Sabrina's. It was locked up to deter any sleight of hand on the still-working device. The Dimensional Device Disruptors were built by the same master who trained both Sabrina and Amelia in their own dimension, designed with an evil purpose to break the rules of dimensional travel and spread evil among the world's patrons. Designed for that and used for … well, you know what they were used for. There isn't concern more can be created, because the man who created the objects has become senile and doesn't recall how he made them.

Jonas explained the watch last, creating a somewhat sentimental moment. The watch was created in Control Dimension 05 many years before the other PDTs displayed here were created. It is regarded as the most successful of the PDTs currently collected because it has been used to do the most damage. I know PDTs aren't meant to do damage, but rather give people the ability to travel without constant approval of the Dimensional Travelers Alliance, but have we seen much good come from them yet? Okay, so Jason and Sabrina did some good with one, but Amelia negated all of their good.

After explaining each of the objects in turn to Jason, Jonas led him out to the main room to see the group still sitting on the couch with Amelia lying on top of their legs. They were watching the Seer Television, peering in on the lives of those around the dimensions.

"Has she conked out yet?" Jonas asked as he briskly walked up to the couch. Upon seeing Amelia fast asleep, he knew the answer. "Good. You all need to watch something. It is incredibly hilarious."

Jonas reached down and took the remote from Trandon. Jason moved over beside Jonas, having hoisted Teddy onto his shoulders. Jonas changed the image on the television to show a recording of

Amelia. She was apparently in her own dimension, dressed in a leather apron and dark clothing. It showed her sticking the retainer in her mouth and then trying to use it but only getting shocked by it. Her mouth went numb because of this. He then fast-forwarded a bit, telling them how much they needed to see this next part. Amelia was now visiting what Jonas pointed out as the Dimensional Travel Point in her home dimension, a giant ceramic cat. She kept trying to pronounce the dimensional numbers while using the Dimensional Device Disruptor, but due to her numb mouth, she wasn't able to announce the numbers and kept traveling to random dimensions. They all laughed at the poor, passed-out Amelia's expense.

"I came across this gem while doing research on Amelia after taking over for my son, seeing as Trandon kept pausing the screen every time she came on it." Jonas looked intensely at Trandon before continuing. "Oh, and excellent job on handing over the watch, Jason. I should've asked Velma to bolt that one to your arm."

Jason shrugged, having no regrets.

"She has talked men into doing worse things …" Sabrina said, trailing off at the end. She had sat down on the couch and was once again her sister's pillow.

Earlier, when Amelia laid down, she opted to have the top half of her sister on her end of the couch, while Trandon was granted Amelia's feet lying across his lap. The young man had become quite infatuated with Amelia, seeing as she actually talked to him, unlike her stepsister.

"I have no doubt." Jonas yawned. "Oh, it is late somewhere. I think it is time to get everyone home, wake the drunkard, and meet downstairs."

Jonas went ahead of them to the stairs and started walking down. Sabrina rudely woke up her stepsister, and Jason helped Sabrina slowly walk Amelia down the stairs. It needs to be clarified that the alcohol Amelia consumed hadn't followed her. She was just tired, and Jonas was picking on her.

At the bottom of the stairs, surrounding the lamp is where they all stood. Amelia was leaning on Sabrina. Amelia kept saying incoherent phrases that revolved around her being woken up and needing to lie back down in her bed. Jonas just smiled and patted her head.

"I thank you for not messing any more things up than you did, Sabrina. Amelia, it was a pleasure to meet you. Perhaps next time you could stay awake. I'm just not sure the conversation would be better," Jonas stated as he reached out an arm and hugged them both. Sabrina gave him a sideways glance and halfway grinned; she then looked over at Jason. He smiled and walked closer, wrapping his arms around her neck in a hug.

Amelia protested that she wasn't a part of the hug and reached out a hand around Jason's back. Jonas watched this display of affection and then quickly whispered something in Trandon's ear. Trandon ran up the stairs.

Jason whispered in Sabrina's ear, "I'll miss you." He pulled back to meet her eyes with his.

"I know you will. Your life won't be the same without me," Sabrina responded, being less quiet than Jason. They then tightly hugged again. Sabrina even wrapped an arm around Jason.

Now that, they had made hugging a new favorite pastime, it was time to split up. Jonas pulled out a sheet of scrap paper from his pocket and handed it to Sabrina. It had the dimensional code that she needed to call out. As she stood there looking at it, Trandon came back down the stairs and handed something to Jonas.

"Well, it has been quite a fun time. Take care of yourself, Jason, Teddy." Sabrina reached out and rubbed the bear's head. Amelia tried to follow suit but only was able to get Jason's nose. "And thank you, Jonas." She reached out her right hand toward Jonas. He shook her hand with a smile.

When she had completed the handshake with Jonas, she looked down at her open hand. In the palm of her hand lay the same ring she had been using for the past few weeks. She looked down at it with an odd look, as if it were the last of things she'd expect ever to see again. To an average person, I'm sure it was like having a piece of jewelry that someone had taken from you returned—a piece of jewelry that had become so meaningful to you that you'd hoard it away in your underwear drawer, hoping no one would look there because it contains your unmentionables, but knowing your luck some pervert would be browsing your dresser drawers and find it. Wait a minute, forget it, I got off of the subject at hand.

"It won't work anymore, but you can keep it as a memento. Besides, Trandon has been complaining about how girly it is to use, so we made him a new one."

Trandon grinned as he showed off the shark's tooth necklace he now wore. Sabrina's eyes narrowed. I'm sure she'd rather have the necklace than the ring.

"Oh, well thanks," Sabrina stated, pocketing the ring. She then reached out an arm and hugged Jonas. Amelia got squished in between them during the hug and made a purring sound for no apparent reason. "Amelia appreciates the gift too." Sabrina then turned to face the lamp and quickly eyed Trandon. He was standing there, arms wide open. She reached out an arm and patted him on the head. "I still don't trust you, kiddo."

Sabrina sighed as she assisted her stepsister down to the floor so that she could grab hold of one of Sabrina's ankles. Sabrina then reached out a hand and touched the lamppost. It only took a couple of seconds for her to read off the code aloud before they were gone. Jason swore within that split second of her finishing the code to disappearing, he saw her give him a sad face.

Teddy was granted a pardon from returning to his dimension and was adopted as a full-time pet by Jonas. It was allowed only because Jason was a Dimensional Warden now and would be making stops in the Seer Dimension; plus, he could take Teddy for walks in random dimensions. So that left Trandon to return home. He had started high school only a week ago, which explains the new lingo and clothing. After watching Trandon depart, Jason and Jonas stood there for a few seconds looking out at the twinkling lights.

"Beautiful, are they not? The stars." Jonas moved over beside Jason and looked out at the stars with him. "This dimension is a peculiar one, isn't it? It is designed so that no matter where you were in another dimension, you'll end up in the same place down here. Also, it was designed with a sort of twilight effect, which usually scares people that stumbled upon it."

A few moments of silence passed as they both looked out at the twinkling stars.

"When we were fixing the dimensional issues, why didn't you have us use the lamppost rather than the watch?" Jason asked Jonas, having this question lingering in his mind for a while.

"A good question!" Jonas placed one of his arms around Jason's shoulders. "Even though the watch had the potential to disrupt dimensional personalities, I could keep it at a minimal. Not to mention, the lamp wouldn't allow me to quickly bring Sabrina back, seeing as she'd travel to a DTP and could do as she pleased in that dimension. With the watch, she would be returned. Now I know she probably could've removed it, but do you think she'd really give it up that easily?" Jonas paused for a moment, turning to face Jason. "Besides, didn't you notice? Even when you were wearing the watch, she came back. I think she got quite attached to you." Jonas laughed as he patted Jason on the back. He then walked to the stairs and went up them. Jason followed behind a bit after, grinning because he knew what Jonas said was true.

When they made it to the top of the stairs, Jonas noticed he still had the remote in his hand and handed it over to Jason. "I plan on taking myself a nap if you want to watch a little television. I'm sure you can figure the remote out. It works off of thought." Jonas walked back into his office and returned to his usual sleeping position, while Jason moved over to the couch.

The remote was actually quite simple. It had one button on it labeled GUIDE. As Jason held on to the remote, he felt a strange connection with the Seer Television, almost as if he had become the remote. That is crazy, right? Jason started out by pushing the giant button on the remote, and as he did so, the screen changed to show a list of options on it. Among these that stood out to him were ALERTS and SEER LOGS.

Jason read in his head *ALERTS*, and as he did, the screen changed to a list of alerts. The list wasn't actually that long. Perhaps they had done an admirable job fixing these issues. Each alert had the dimension in which the alarm was triggered, the possible perpetrator, the problem caused, and the option to view a clip.

Jason, using his mind, was able to move the cursor on the television screen to select an action. He decided to choose the third from the top, no real reason why. The television changed to show someone using a shovel to beat on a mailbox. He was cursing it for not letting him through. It wasn't smart of the man to do such a thing, because within seconds of smashing the shovel into the mailbox, it electrocuted him. He went flying backward, landing hard on the ground. The video stopped there. Jason assumed the mailbox was a malfunctioning Dimensional Travel Point. He'd let Jonas deal with this one.

After moments had passed, he thought of what he wanted to see next, his mind racing with different possibilities. All the while, the Seer Television changed to depict whatever he thought he wanted to see. Finally, it stopped on Sabrina. He wasn't paying attention to the television, and it wasn't until he heard her voice that he freaked out. Jason had been in deep thought, imagining how Sabrina was doing even though she had only returned home a few minutes ago.

He looked at the television. It showed Sabrina assisting Amelia down onto a bed in what looked to be a rather ordinary, messy apartment. She then walked sleepily into her own room, crashed on her bed, and then thumbed over the opal ring a few times before setting it on her nightstand. Sabrina started to pull clothes off while under her sheets, which made Jason slightly embarrassed, so he quickly thought of something else, and the television focused on Trandon instead. Why'd he think that? The television showed Trandon arriving at his home and talking to his mom. She asked about his weekend, and he was exceedingly apathetic toward her. It was all standard teenage stuff.

Jason had almost put the remote down when his mind wandered to something else. The television switched views to accommodate this change in thought and showed the Seer Logs, precisely the ones when he was displaced to the Opposite Dimension. He sat there for a few minutes, wanting to see what happened to his body whenever he had left to a different dimension. He wanted to know who took it over, what he did, and what was said.

"No, I don't want to feel embarrassed." He put the remote down on the armrest and looked over at Teddy, who had now covered himself with a blanket and was sleeping on the other side of the couch. Jason watched the little bear for a few moments before hearing thundering snores come from the room behind him. Jason felt the tiredness too, so he tapped his watch and thought in his mind *Control Dimension 05.* The screen lit up and displayed the dimension he thought, he then touched the screen again, and as he did, it only took a second before he was gone from the Seer Dimension.

Chapter 13

Months had passed since Jason had taken on his first real job. He had to explain to his uncle about leaving his fake job at the video store, which ended with his uncle in tears. His parents were proud of him when he didn't request gas money and handled it himself. They hadn't talked to him much about all the crazy shenanigans that went on when he was jumping dimensions. They'd crack some jokes, but for the most part, they looked happy.

Cara had begun a new relationship, so she was rarely around to pester Jason, and he wasn't around to be pestered. He has caught her coming home at the wee hours of the morning even though he too was returning home that late. I imagine his parents don't think he has the willpower to do anything wrong, so they wouldn't care even if he were gone until the morning. It's not that they wouldn't care at all. You read about the hospital. They were there.

Jason woke up on a cool day; it was winter, and he actually wore a shirt and pants to bed now. The convenience of his new job was that he wasn't required to be up at any particular time. The inconvenience of his job was that Jonas had to modify his watch to make an alarm noise whenever Jason was being summoned because he had missed a few notifications.

Jason stretched out under the covers of his bed, staring up at his ceiling. There he lay, thinking about other ways he could improve his life. After all, he was now waking up before ten in the morning. It had crossed his mind more than a few times to go back to college, so he lay there debating it again. He was making a good sum of money, and his time was sporadic but allowed for online courses. What was the holdup? Perhaps it was that he wasn't sure what degree to pursue.

After a few more moments in thought, Jason sat up in his bed and yawned. His room had not changed much, save from him finally replacing the broken picture frame that contained the battle hero painting. He laughed upon seeing it.

"I too would've loved to jump into that one," he said quietly to himself before hearing the meowing of his family's door mat cat.

The cat, Bingles, was being allowed inside during the colder months. It immediately jumped onto Jason's bed, taking his warm spot on the covers.

Jason stood up after petting Bingles and walked to the bathroom. While standing in front of the mirror after using the restroom, Jason peered at himself deeply. He felt alone for some reason even though he was far from alone and even further from depression.

Eventually, Jason got over his moment of pity and dressed himself, grabbing his keys, wallet, and watch. He had planned to have lunch with the Sabrina from his dimension. They had been hanging out again without too many details being spread in regards to the dimensions. She had practically chalked the whole experience up to a pleasant dream, seeing as no one believed her and Jason remained quiet on the subject.

The drive to the mall brought many emotions back to Jason. He had driven it hundreds of times. Even when he was first helping the Evil-Plotters Dimension Sabrina out, he was driving it, but for some reason, this trip felt the oddest. The feeling of missing something lingered deep in him.

Eventually, he made it to the mall and inside of it. He left the vehicle outside of the mall, just to clarify.

Inside the mall, he found Sabrina waiting at Trendno, where she looked as interested in everything as she normally did.

"Hey, Jason, come to get me out of this hell?" Sabrina said with a sigh. I'm sure she meant the empty store was hell because there was nothing else going on around her.

"Yeah, what do you want for food?" Jason asked.

"I don't care. Let's walk up to the food court and just sample things." Sabrina walked out from behind the Trendno store counter and then past Jason.

He followed her out of the store and then walked beside her.

"You ever think you want to do more than work at a store in the mall?" Jason asked Sabrina, putting more confidence into his words than he usually would when talking to her.

"So now that you got a good job, you are looking down on me? You are just like my stepdad! First trying to get me to go to college, and now he is attempting to get me a job at his workplace!"

"No, no. I didn't mean it that way!"

"It is whatever." She calmed down quickly from her outburst. "I know you don't believe me, and no else does, but I want to live with that crazy old man and the guy with the shrunken arm. I had more fun plotting all of those plans than I've had in my whole life!"

Jason didn't disagree with this. He knew she didn't have a very exciting life, and after a few moments, a way to fix this crossed his mind.

"Sabrina, I don't work for a software company programming from home," Jason said, stopping Sabrina and placing a hand on either of her shoulders so that they faced each other.

Sabrina looked at him with a confused look on her face.

"I'm a Dimensional Warden."

Sabrina's eyes opened wide. "Are you serious?"

Jason dropped his arms from Sabrina's shoulders and furrowed his brows. He was clearly unsure if what she said was meant to be sarcastic.

"The shrunken-arm man told me about Dimensional Wardens! He said that they gave him a hard time because of the watch he made." Sabrina had gotten excited. Way more excited than Jason had ever seen. She then glanced down at the watch on his wrist. "Is that one like the one he had?"

Jason nodded his head, still in disbelief.

"Okay! I'll grab onto your arm, and we'll be off!" Sabrina said, grabbing hold of Jason's right arm.

"Well, uh … I mean, you can take my arm, but ankles are better for dimensional traveling," Jason said, hoping he knew at least one thing that she didn't on this subject.

Sabrina snorted. "The shrunken-arm guy told me that is a myth! Plus it is a little demeaning, Jason. I'm not giving into my stepdad's ridiculous idea of paying for me to go to college, and I won't let you talk me into grabbing your ankle."

Jason tapped the screen of his calculator watch before contemplating what he was doing. This girl is crazy. Should he be doing this? He did miss the other dimensional personality of Sabrina.

"Yeah, yours is way cooler than the watch the shrunken-arm guy explained was his."

"Do you not remember his name?" Jason asked before thinking, *Evil-Plotters Dimension.* The text came up on the watch's screen.

"Who cares? The guy spent most of his time crying and working on his evil look. Let's go!" Sabrina reached over, tapping the screen on Jason's watch, and they were both pulled through the floor and into another dimension.

Jason had only visited this dimension once before and realized it hadn't changed much. There was still much darkness, explosions, and cackling going on. He looked to his right, where Sabrina had been grabbing hold of his arm and noticed she wasn't there. In fact, she was getting up off the ground a good way away from him. From there, she waved to Jason and started running off, cackling the whole way.

A question that might be asked at this point would be "How does Jason know where he is at in this dimension? The new watch doesn't swap personalities, so where does he go?" Well, the watch has an answer for that. It is where Jason wills it. Much like bringing objects with him when using the watch, he can will where he wants to go. There are accuracy issues, but at least it does more than tell the time!

Jason had willed himself to appear near somewhere, a place where Sabrina could run free and he could visit an old friend. I realize I'm trying to be cryptic, but I'm sure you all know where we are going with this.

As he walked toward a bench, one that sat facing a large apartment building, he saw who he was looking for. He knew she'd be around here because her apartment was close. Also, she would probably be outside of the apartment, seeing as it was subjected to many evildoers' mischievous plans and once even her own. She was staring at a piece of paper, wearing clothes very similar to what she'd had on in the Seer Dimension. To him, she looked lovely even though her face was covered in black powder and she had a pair of oversized goggles on top of her head.

"What are you reading?" Jason asked, having snuck up behind the Evil-Plotters Dimension Sabrina.

Sabrina shifted in her seat, not looking at Jason. Jason looked at the crumpled paper in her hand. It was a list of dimensional codes. He wasn't sure which ones exactly, but they seemed oddly familiar. They were probably from one of the dimensional jumps when Jason and Sabrina were fixing mishaps. I don't even remember.

"Nothing important," Sabrina responded after her brief moment of silence.

Jason, feeling taken aback from her lack of noticing who he was, took a seat next to her. Sabrina turned her head to see Jason.

"Jonas sending you on errands?"

"No. I came here because I wanted to see you."

"Well, if all you wanted to do is see me, you should have just hung around with my other dimensional personality from the freak store," Sabrina stated, turning her head away from Jason.

Jason was speechless. He sat there dumbfounded for a few moments before he heard Sabrina chuckle.

"Could you imagine me really being like that?" she asked, turning to face Jason with a grin.

"No. Not at all."

"Good," Sabrina leaned in and kissed Jason on his lips, locking for a brief period of time before releasing, "because I'd probably punch you."

Jason laughed before placing his hand behind Sabrina's head, pulling her in for a deeper kiss. This went on for a few minutes, but I'll spare you the details.

"Come back with me," Jason said after they finished their kissing.

"How? I mean, I know you have the new watch, but I might run into the Sabrina from your dimension."

"Not a chance." Jason averted his eyes to the area behind Sabrina, where not too far past the bench they were on stood Amelia, who was talking with the shrunken-arm guy and the Sabrina from Control Dimension 05.

Sabrina traced Jason's eyes to the spot where he was looking and then turned back to him with a smile, something he hadn't often seen.

"Well. I'm going to ask you one last question then." She reached down and lifted up Jason's right leg, placing it on her lap. "Where to?"

Jason smiled back at her, tapping the watch on his wrist.

"I have the perfect place in mind."

Jason tapped the screen again, and they were gone.

EPILOGUE

———— ❖ ————

So you see now how this book can help you. As a possible accidental dimensional traveler, you should have a better understanding of dimensional travel.

Jason has done a great job of being an example for future accidental dimensional travelers. Even though I don't agree with what he did with the two Sabrinas, because I would have left them both in the Evil-Plotters Dimension. Yet I understand Jason and Sabrina are in some sort of love, the kind that confuses everyone who tries to talk to you about it.

Anyway, to tie up one last loose end, allow me to introduce myself. My name is Jonas. Oh, you already knew that, didn't you? Well, aren't we special?

Whatever—I am happy that you took the time to read this because if you do find yourself traveling through dimensions, you shall now be better prepared. And if while traveling through these dimensions you ever find a Personal Dimensional Transporter somewhere, please be sure to try to use it. That way we can track you down, retrieve the lost item, and return you back to your proper dimension. Don't worry about us spoiling your fun because you'll have plenty of tales to tell so that people think you are crazy.

Thank you,
Jonas

Printed in the United States
By Bookmasters